SECRET PROTECTOR

SECRET TEMPTATIONS BOOK 2

CAMERON HART

*

Jasper: Faye is easily the most beautiful woman I've ever seen. She's also stuck-up, spoiled, and my new stepsister.

As a lawyer, I'm good at reading people. Faye has perfect hair, perfect clothes, and a perfect, cushy little life. Or so I thought.

Beneath her well-honed facade, is a woman who longs for acceptance, love, and intimacy. I've never been very good at any of those things, but I'm a quick learner.

I don't care if she's my stepsister. I'd do anything for Faye, my broken little pixie.

Faye: Jasper is a jerk. A hot jerk, but a jerk nonetheless. Oh, and he's my new stepbrother. He sees my designer shoes and pricey handbags and thinks he knows me. Everyone does. They don't know the real price of living my life.

When it all becomes too much for me to take, Jasper is there with a shoulder to cry on. I shouldn't trust his sweet words and gentle touches. I shouldn't ache for more.

I shouldn't want my stepbrother, but I'm already in too deep.

WANT A FREE BOOK?

Sign up for my newsletter and get your copy of Chasing Stacy.

River: One look at the stunning waitress carrying the weight of the world on her shoulders, and I'm a gonner. I wasn't looking for a sweet little thing with auburn hair and more baggage than I can fit on the back of my bike, but there's no going back now. She's mine. I'll prove to her I'm more than capable of handling her past and making her feel safe again.

CONNECT WITH ME!

Check out my website, camoronhart.net, for sneak previews on my latest projects.

Follow me on social media:
  Facebook Page
  Facebook Group
  Instagram
  TikTok
  Goodreads
  Bookbub

Sign up for my street team to receive ARCs & help spread the word about new releases.

CHAPTER ONE

JASPER

"**W**atch it!" I grumble, laying on the horn as a sleek, silver Mercedes Coupe slams on its breaks ahead of me and then guns it, swerving into the left lane. Fucking NYC traffic. I swear everyone is out to murder each other as soon as they get behind the wheel in this goddamn city.

I take the first exit off the freeway into Manhattan, rolling my shoulders to break up the tension in my muscles from the nerve-wracking drive. I'm headed to La Amis to meet my dad and his new wife. Of course, the woman he chose to marry would want to dine at the most pretentious restaurant. La Amis is one of the top bistros in the city and a favorite for the key players in high society, which Monica certainly is.

Monica Carmichael. Or Monica Thorn, now that they've tied the knot. The two of them met while my father was conducting business in the Hamptons. Monica was having a lavish getaway weekend, and my father spotted her lying out on the beach during his lunch break. They were married by the end of the week and broke the news about the arrangement to their families only yesterday. Hence, I'm going to meet her for the first time tonight. I'm still reeling from the shock, but my father is adamant that it's true love. Yeah, right.

The idea of love was ruined for me the moment my mom walked out. I was eleven, and my father had just been diagnosed with cancer. It was too much for her to handle. That's all she said. I guess I was also too much for her. My mother had her bags packed and the divorce papers drawn up before the first round of chemo started.

I glance at the clock on my dashboard, cursing under my breath when I see it's already five past six. I hate being late. As a lawyer, time is money. That's why I'm the first to arrive at the office and the last to leave. I'm punctual for every hour in between.

Maybe my tardiness is subconscious. I'd be lying if I said I wasn't dreading this dinner.

I want my father to be happy and fulfilled, but I don't think getting married was the right move. That's why I did some digging into his new wife's history. This isn't her first marriage. In fact, it's not her second, third, or fourth. Monica has a trail of ex-husbands, and dead husbands, who add to her wealth via alimony and life insurance policies. I'm not sure what she sees in my dad since he doesn't make nearly the kind of money her ex-husbands have in the past.

Dad and I make a decent amount of money, running our law firm, Thorn & Thorn. After my dad kicked cancer's ass, we both had a wake-up call. He didn't want to be a middle manager anymore, and as an impressionable teen who'd just watched his dad beat cancer, I wanted to do whatever he wanted to do.

We studied together, went to college together, passed the bar together, and opened our own practice together. You could say my dad is my best friend, which wouldn't be wrong. Not that we ever talk about it. I know he worries that I don't have anyone else in my life. But I don't need anyone. I've seen the kind of devastation relationships can have on a person, and I'm not interested in drama. No, thank you. I'll stick to facts, laws, and running the firm.

My GPS directs me to pull into the restaurant, and I turn the wheel, just in time to see a silver car cut me off in line. I slam on my brakes and honk, only to see a perfectly manicured hand stick out the window and flip me off.

"Unbelievable," I growl. It's the same Mercedes Coupe from the freeway. I sit in my car, stewing angrily about the woman who nearly caused an accident for the second time today. Typical spoiled brat.

I watch her step out of her car and toss her keys to the valet before combing her fingers through her long black hair and straightening her dress. I try pulling my eyes away from her, but I can't. She's enchanting. *No, she's high maintenance*, I correct myself.

So what if her silky hair would look good wrapped around my fist while I yank her head back and kiss down her neck? It doesn't matter that her curves are giving me all kinds of filthy ideas. My eyes wander down her body without my permission, drinking in every inch of her frame, from the top of her head to the tips of her painted toenails.

A loud honk jolts me from my stupor, and I realize I'm holding up the valet line. I shake my head and pull up, putting the car in park before handing my keys to the valet.

Standing outside the restaurant, I take a few deep breaths and brace myself for what's inside. The sound of heels clicking on the cement fills my head, along with the delicate scent of roses and something sweet. I've never smelled it before.

I turn to see who's approaching me, then narrow my eyes when I see it's *her*. The little road warrior herself. I'm frozen in place, and apparently, I've forgotten how to speak. She lifts an eyebrow at me, letting me see her eyes for the first time up close. What color is that? It's not quite blue, but it can't be purple, can it? I didn't even know eyes came in that color.

My throat is dry, and I try unsticking my tongue from the roof of my mouth so I don't just stand here gaping at her. However, she turns on her heel before I can get a word out. My jaw hangs open, and dammit, I can't help but stare at her ass as it sways back and forth in her royal blue cocktail dress. Those five-inch red pumps she's wearing aren't helping me keep my dirty thoughts to myself. Now all I can picture is this sexy creature wearing nothing but those shoes while I drag my lips all over her skin.

Fucking get it together, man!

What the hell is wrong with me? I've never been distracted by women, let alone a singular woman. Especially if she's entitled and drives like shit.

The enchantress tosses her hair over her shoulder as she turns to look at me. "If you're gonna check out the goods, you might as well hold the door open for me."

My jaw snaps shut, my teeth clanging together painfully. Who does she think she is? And more importantly, why does she fluster me so much? I spend long days in courtrooms with immense pressure, but one look from those purple eyes has me all out of sorts.

I'm about to tell her off, but instead, I watch my hand reach out for the door and pull it open, stepping to the side to let her through.

"I guess chivalry isn't dead, after all. Just horny," she muses.

That does it. My throat loosens, and I find my voice. "I'm not–"

The sassy, spoiled woman in red pumps is already walking away. She heads straight inside, not bothering to stop and talk to the hostess. Rude. I watch her weave around tables like she owns the place. For all I know, her family might. She certainly looks like she's not hurting for money.

I have to make a concentrated effort to pull my eyes away from her curvy figure, but I manage it somehow. Addressing the hostess, I let her know I'm meeting family here. I give her my father's name, Conner Thorn, and follow her through the restaurant.

I may have a good job now with steady cash flow and big, fat bank accounts, but it wasn't always that way. My dad and I worked our asses off to build Thorn & Thorn. Being in places like this, with honest-to-god gold trim painted on the crown molding, always makes me antsy. This restaurant feels more like a medieval castle with fresh flowers on all the tables, low candlelight, gaudy paintings of half-naked men and women, velvet drapes, and golden accents. I can't imagine why anyone would want that as an aesthetic, but the fame of La Amis proves me wrong.

I've been in these socialite circles for over a decade now. I've probably represented several people in this very room. I specialize in real estate litigation, and if there's one thing I've learned, it's that rich people are *very* territorial.

Business is good but I'm still not used to the flashy life-style of millionaires. I guess I better get ready, and fast because I'm about to meet one.

The hostess stops in front of a booth, holding her hand out to show me that this is my party. I nod at my father, who's wearing a crispy, black suit, looking sharp as ever with his closely cropped hair and spectacles. Glancing over at Monica, I give what I hope is a smile but I'm cringing on the inside.

She looks exactly like I pictured; fake, from the botox in her lips to the extensions in her hair. She lifts her hand, presenting it to me as if she's a queen and I'm her subject.

Does she expect me to kiss her hand or some shit? Not going to happen. Instead, I grab her hand in an awkward hand-shake. She balks at my apparent rudeness but doesn't say anything.

I hear a muffled laugh and turn my attention to the other side of the booth. My eyes land on another woman sitting across from them.

Purple eyes widen in shock as they stare up at me.

What the hell is she doing here?

"Jasper, I'd like you to meet Faye. Your new stepsister."

CHAPTER TWO

FAYE

I *t's him.* The jerk who honked at me twice on my way over to the restaurant.

What is he doing here? I gape at him, ignoring his slightly messy sandy brown hair and sharp green eyes. I also ignore his stubble, and I absolutely don't think about how it would feel scraping against my cheek. My neck. My thighs...

Get it together!

Is he here to yell at me? Call me out for insulting his delicate sensibilities? Maybe I should regret my comment about chivalry not being dead, but I don't. He deserved it for checking me out. Never mind that I may have put a little extra sashay into my step. It's not like I thought he was actually going to take the bait.

I'm a big girl with wide hips and more than a little junk in my trunk. Not many guys know how to handle all my curves. Then again, it's not like I know, either. I haven't done so much as kiss a guy, and at twenty-one, that's unheard of.

"Faye!" my mom snaps, giving me a severe look. Or, I think she is. My mother recently had another Botox treatment, so her facial expressions all look the same. Her dark blue eyes flash dangerously, though, and I know I'm on thin ice. "Say hello to your stepbrother, for goodness sake."

That's when it hits me. *Stepbrother*? This asshat?

I choke out a cough, then grab my glass of water, chugging it down. The whole time, the muscled, green-eyed Greek god stares at me with an unreadable look. His charcoal gray suit fits him perfectly, the material snug against the contours of his beefy biceps and wide shoulders. Not that I'm paying attention to any of that.

"Hi," I squeak out, instantly cringing at how childish I sound. I'm making great impressions left and right with this guy, which would bother me if I cared. As it is, my mom will probably drop her latest husband, like all the others in her long line of gold-digging conquests.

My mother rolls her eyes, obviously displeased with me. What else is new?

"Faye, this is Jasper," she says with clear exasperation in her voice.

"I'm Faye," I say stupidly, realizing too late my mother has already introduced me.

The arrogant man smirks at me, holding out his hand. I narrow my eyes at him, then hear my mom clearing her throat, not so subtly urging me to shake his hand.

"Jasper," he replies, his voice deep and velvety.

My hand slides into his, and a shiver runs down my spine. His touch sparks something inside me, something I can't think about at the moment. It's probably just stress. And shock. Yes, this whole week has been a shock, ever since my mom returned from her vacation with a ring on her finger and a husband hanging on her every word.

"Honestly, Faye, I don't know what's gotten into you tonight. Scoot over so Jasper can sit down."

My anger flares at Mom's scolding whisper. If she's not talking down to me or treating me like my existence is a burden, then she's nitpicking my clothes, my weight, or anything else that isn't up to her standards.

I move over, clinging to the wall and wishing it would open up so I could disappear. I hate these dinners. Any dinner with my mom, really, but especially the dinners where I'm meeting her flavor of the month.

I'll admit, this husband confuses me. Conner isn't poor by any stretch of the imagination, but he's not the biggest fish my mom has caught, either. She likes her husbands flush with cash and, preferably, on the brink of death. Okay, that's a little extreme. Only two of her husbands have died of old age. Her first husband, my father, also died, but… well, I can't think about that right now.

A peppermint and pine scent invades my senses, and then he's right here, next to me. Jasper's warm, commanding presence is overwhelming, and I hold my breath to keep my head from spinning.

Thankfully, the waiter comes and saves me from another awful interaction.

"Have we decided on beverages for the evening?" the middle-aged man in a tuxedo asks. "May I suggest the *Buccella Mica Cabernet?*"

Conner and the waiter talk about vintages and vineyards, and my eyes start to glaze over. Even though I've had a luxurious lifestyle since I was seven, I still don't understand how people can spend a thousand dollars on wine and a meal.

"Cat got your tongue?" Jasper whispers.

I startle, looking over at him. He's leaned in closer, much closer than I thought, and I get caught up in his green eyes as they stare at me, a spark of challenge lurking in their depths.

"No," I counter, crossing my arms.

Jasper's eyes dart down to my chest before he catches himself.

I smirk, then wink when he looks back up at me.

"Sorry," he mumbles, clearing his throat.

I shrug, knowing it makes my breasts bounce. His jaw clenches, and I can't help the grin on my face as he turns to face our parents.

"Faye, I was just telling Conner about your studies," my mom says, bringing me into the conversation.

"Really?" That's surprising. I didn't think my mom even knew what my major was.

"Yes, that one class about classical art."

"That was two years ago, and I only took it to fulfill a humanity credit," I say flatly.

"Still," she persists. "It was the most interesting one, I think. Conner and I are going to get into art collecting. Maybe you could help us pick out a few pieces."

It might sound like a nice offer, but I know my mom. She always has an agenda. "It's not really my area of interest," I hedge, not wanting to set my mother off in public. "If you want to discuss landscaping or cross-pollination–"

"That's alright, Faye," my mom cuts me off, waving her hand in the air to dismiss my comment.

I grip my spoon tightly in my fist, fantasizing about using it as a trebuchet to fling ice in her face.

The conversation moves on, my mother asking Jasper about his role as partner at Thorn & Thorn. Fine. Good. I'm too worked up to have a civil discussion anyway. I hate the way she always tries to shove me into a mold of the perfect daughter. She hates that I have what she calls a "man's degree," so she refuses to bring it up, focusing instead on art classes or something becoming of a young woman in high society.

Fuck that.

However, I'm still living under my mom's roof, so it's best for me to bite my tongue until I graduate and move out.

Jasper's knee grazes mine, and I jerk my head in his direction. The man tips his chin up, avoiding eye contact. I don't know what comes over me, but I pull away from the contact then hit his knee with mine.

I study his profile, a wicked sense of pleasure coursing through me when the corner of his lip curves up. Those green eyes dart over to mine, a barely perceptible glint lighting them up from the inside.

"And, for you, miss?"

I look up, noticing for the first time that our waiter has returned for our orders. Good thing I eat here often since I didn't crack the menu once. "I'll have Chicken Francese with a side of roasted potatoes."

"Are you sure you don't want the Mediterranean salad, dear?" my mother asks, giving me a pointed look.

"Nope," I answer, popping the "p" obnoxiously. "I'm a chicken and potatoes kind of girl, no sense in trying to hide it."

The waiter looks between my mother and me, then hastily writes down my order, moving on to Jasper next. A pointy object stabs me from under the table, and I look at my mom. She's kicking my shins with her pointed heels and giving me a withering glare. I pretend not to notice, focusing on my water, which has suddenly become the most interesting thing in the world.

It's not the first time my mother has made a dig at my weight, nor will it be the last. I tell myself her opinion doesn't matter, that her insults come from a shallow, lonely place inside of her, and say more about her as a person than me. Most days, I even convince myself her hurtful words make me stronger. Today, however, I'm feeling extra vulnerable and out of sorts. As much as I don't want to admit it, I think my new stepbrother has something to do with that.

The rest of dinner is a mix of awkward tension and back-handed compliments from my mom. It's pretty obvious I don't trust her new beau and his son, and for his part, Jasper doesn't seem to trust my mom or me. Fair enough. I just want this night to be over. Soon, their marriage will be over as well. Then I won't have to deal with Jasper anymore.

Conner pays for dinner, and I thank him. Manners were beaten into me, sometimes literally, but mostly through scolding and unreasonable punishments when I messed up to ensure I wouldn't make the same mistake twice. Ever since I turned eighteen three years ago, though, I've started branching out a little more.

The four of us make our way outside, heading to the valet. Mom and Conner inform us they're going down the street for a nightcap and will get their car later. We say our goodbyes, and then it's just Jasper and me.

I glance over at him, but he's looking straight ahead. Does he feel this weird vibe between us? I don't like him, that's for sure. But I also... I don't know. I'm not done with him yet, but I don't know what else I want from my arrogant step-brother.

My car pulls up, followed by Jasper's. He motions me to go first, and I give him a strange look. He smirks at me, and I don't know if I want to slap him or rub myself against him. Dammit.

"I figured I'd let you go first. That way, there's less of a chance you'll cut me off."

I give him my best glare, clenching my teeth so hard they ache. He simply grins, which infuriates me further. "Try not to look at my ass when I walk away," I grumble, making him chuckle. I can't decide if I hate that sound or love it.

The valet hops out of the car, and I slide in his place,

slamming the door and rolling down the window. I peel out of the restaurant, middle finger hanging out the window. Glancing in my rearview mirror, I catch the amused look on Jasper's face. It takes an admirable amount of self-control not to put my car in reverse and smash the front of his shiny black BMW, but I manage to keep driving forward. My mom would be so proud.

CHAPTER THREE

JASPER

"Yes, Mr. Cross, I have been notified about the latest update concerning the Mansfield property, and I'm working on a defense," I say for the third time during this phone call.

My client, Mr. Cross, is in a fierce property war with another land owner. They keep wanting to redraw lines around the two pieces of land, claiming their great-great-great grand-something originally owned it. Possession is nine-tenths of the law, so if that's true, I've got an uphill battle.

"Well, what are you planning to do about it?" he screeches.

I pull the phone away from my ear, taking a deep breath and running my free hand through my hair. I tug at the strands, hoping the sting will wake me up enough to get through this damn call. I've been sleeping like shit this last week, and it's all thanks to one Miss Faye Charmichael.

"If I had a defense prepared, we'd be talking about that instead of this," I mutter. "I have to go, Mr. Cross. We'll be in touch soon." I hang up before he gets a chance to ask me more pointless questions.

I need to get my shit together. This whole week has been a sleep-deprived blur. It started that first night after meeting Faye. I couldn't get her out of my head, no matter how many rounds with the punching bag I did or how hard I pushed myself on the weights. The adrenaline, sweat, and my elevated heart rate only seemed to make the problem worse.

All I could picture was making Faye sweat as she writhed underneath me, her black hair spread out on my crisp, white sheets. I imagined all the ways I could get her worked up, get her heart beating as fast as mine.

After two hours, I called it quits and resigned myself to a restless night of sleep. Rinse and repeat for six days, and yeah, I'm more of a grumpy asshole than usual.

I lean back in my chair and swivel so I'm looking out the window. Up here on the thirty-eighth floor, I can see the sprawl of New York City. Other skyscrapers partially block my view, but I can still make out people scurrying around like ants, carrying out their duties. Cars zip by, and bikes weave in and out of pedestrians. It looks like complete chaos, but somehow, it all works like cogs spinning in a well-oiled machine.

A knock on the door pulls me from my thoughts, and I spin around to see my father poke his head in. "Am I interrupting anything?"

"No, come on in."

He steps inside my office, leaving the door open. My old man leaves his door open to try and be more accessible and approachable. Not like me. I'd lock my door if I thought I could get away with it.

"Are you doing alright, Son?" he asks, worry creasing his brow. We share the same sandy brown hair, though his is mostly salt-and-pepper. His green eyes match mine, filled with concern.

I wave him off. There's no way in hell I'm telling my father about my secret filthy thoughts about my own goddamn stepsister. "I'm fine, just had a rough week of sleep. I'm sure it'll pass."

He nods his head, though I know he doesn't fully believe me. Thankfully, he lets it slide, leaning into my excuse. "The Mansfield case again?"

I sigh and nod, grateful to have something else to talk about. "Yeah, it just got more complicated. Now the family who owns the property next door is saying they have a deed that belonged to some old relative, stating that one-third of the Mansfield property is rightfully theirs."

"Shit," my dad says.

I grunt in agreement.

"Listen, we can work on it together after lunch. Do you want to join me?" he asks.

The clicking of heels against the marble tiles punctuates the otherwise quiet office environment. A moment later, I'm assaulted by a strong perfume, something expensive and overwhelming. Monica comes charging into my office like she's the queen of the castle. She might have married my father, but this is *my* kingdom.

"There you are!" Monica says in an extra saccharine voice. "I was looking all over for you." She makes her way to my dad, leaning in to kiss him on the cheek. Her red lipstick leaves a mark on his skin, which she rubs off affectionately. She might play the part of a doting wife, but I know she's got some kind of agenda. Women like her always do.

"I was just trying to convince Jasper to come out to lunch with us."

A flash of annoyance slips through Monica's facade, but

she quickly schools her expression. "Of course, what a wonderful idea!"

"No, thank you," I decline. I straighten up some papers on my desk, then grab a folder and start flipping through it, trying to look busy. No way in hell am I going to spend more time with this viper than I have to.

My dad frowns, and I know what's coming next. "You really need to have a life outside of the office, Jasper."

I nod but continue to flip through random files as if I'm looking for something.

"When's the last time you took a lunch break? Or went home early?" he continues.

"I find fulfillment in my work," I tell him, just like every other time he brings this up. He's about to fight me on it, but Monica starts tapping her foot, her ridiculous heels making a sharp, incessant sound.

"Alright," he finally concedes. Turning to Monica, my dad holds out his arm. She takes it and smiles up at him. "Now, to introduce my new wife to the rest of the office," he says.

The two of them leave, not bothering to shut the door. Figures.

I wipe my hands down my face, then rub my eyes, wincing as I feel a headache coming on. A light tap on my door makes me look up. Speaking of headaches, Faye waltzes into my office without asking permission.

"Hey," she says with a mischievous grin.

It shouldn't make me hard, but fuck if I'm not tenting my pants already. I give her a curt nod, scooting closer to my desk to hide my erection. What the hell? Why is my body responding like this to the spoiled little brat?

"Rough day at work?" she asks, walking around the perimeter of my office. Her delicate fingers brush against the books on my shelf, and suddenly all I can picture is her dragging her fingers over my skin, teasing me and...

A loud crash fills the room, and my eyes snap toward Faye. She dropped a paperweight that was on my bookshelf, scuffing both the floor and the marble weight.

"Oops," she says insincerely, shrugging her shoulders. She picks up the heavy thing, blows it off, and sets it back on the shelf as if she didn't just violate my privacy and damage my property.

"To what do I owe this great pleasure?" I ask sarcastically as I focus on my computer. I can't look at her. Can't give her any attention. Her addictive floral scent is already getting on everything, and I know I'll be smelling her for the rest of the day. That shouldn't please me, but it does.

"Just checking out my bro's place of work."

Faye continues to circle the room, finally stopping at one of the floor-to-ceiling windows. She folds her arms over her stomach, almost in a protective hold. In this moment, she looks a little lost. Fragile, almost. The midday sun is bright and warm, coating her in golden light.

"Is it up to your standards?" I snap, forcing myself to look somewhere else. Anywhere else. Before I do something crazy like hold Faye against my chest and curl myself around her to protect her from whatever put that sad look in her purple eyes.

Faye snorts out a laugh. It shouldn't be adorable, dammit.

"Yeah, I'd say you've done pretty well for yourself." I can fucking feel her step up behind me, her scent filling my lungs. "Whatcha working on?" she asks casually, leaning over me to stare at my computer.

"Ever heard of lawyer-client confidentiality?" I growl, turning my screen away from her.

"Jeez, if I didn't know any better, I'd think you were looking at porn or something."

I choke out a cough, then glare at her.

She smirks at me. "Wow, it was some really filthy porn,

huh?"

"No."

"Just normal porn then?"

"Stop saying porn," I grunt.

"Oh, right," she whispers. "We wouldn't want anyone to know about your little indiscretion. Don't worry. Your secret is safe with me."

"Faye," I say in a low, warning tone. She has no fucking clue what my real secret is. My real thoughts. They certainly are filthy, but there's no porn star involved. Only Faye. My goddamn stepsister.

"Fine, fine, I get it. You're not in a joking mood."

I bark out a dry laugh. I can't remember the last time I was in a "joking mood." Faye smiles, her eyes sparkling with something pure and genuine. It's like she enjoyed making me laugh. She certainly enjoys pushing all my buttons, at the very least.

"You better go find your mother. You're all going to lunch soon, so I've been told."

"Trying to get rid of me?" Faye walks around to the front of my desk, putting her hands on her hips. Her wide hips that would feel so damn good in my hands as I pull her toward me and finally claim those cherry red lips.

"So you do pick up on subtle hints," I quip. I'm not having fun. I'm just playing her game to get her out of here.

Keep telling yourself that, buddy.

"Well, I certainly like subtlety over obnoxious honking, if that's what you're getting at." She lifts an eyebrow and curls up one corner of her lips.

Fucking hell, I want to kiss that look off her face. I want to show her what else she can do with that sassy little mouth of hers. "You can't seriously be upset at me for your reckless driving."

"Hey, this is NYC, baby! You gotta be assertive to survive."

"Being assertive is different from committing vehicular homicide."

Faye laughs, the rich sound soothing every part of me. I'm momentarily frozen in place, caught up in the gravity of her joy. She's glowing, her black hair fluttering as she tips her head back. She laughs with her whole body, letting it consume her. How is she so pure and feisty at the same time?

"I'll keep that in mind. If I end up needing a lawyer for my driving escapades, do you know where I can find a good one?"

I glare at her, not allowing any emotion to cross my face as I stare at her beauty. Her eyes are sparkling like she's enjoying our little back and forth. I sure as hell am. Far more than I should.

"No lawyer wants to take on a hit and run involving a crazy chick," I mutter. I think I might have gone too far, but then Faye laughs again. I ignore the ache in my chest, as well as the feeling of emptiness when her laughter stops.

"Are you sure you don't want to go to lunch with us? Sounds like someone is hangry."

"You better get going then. Wouldn't want to see you on the road when you're *assertively* searching for food."

"I meant *you*! You're hangry!"

"Mmhm," I say dismissively, looking back down at my computer screen.

Faye huffs out a breath, and I watch her from the corner of my eye as she spins on her heel and stomps toward the door.

"Close it on your way out," I call.

She growls and slams the door shut. I can't help but grin when she gets all worked up like that.

I don't know about being hangry, but I'm definitely hungry. Food isn't what I long for, though. Only Faye will satiate me. In other words, I'm fucked.

CHAPTER FOUR

FAYE

I close my laptop and rub my temples, trying to massage away the dull headache from staring at the screen for the last four hours. This paper is going to kill me. I've been trying to write about the rarest kinds of orchids found in North America, but I can't concentrate.

It's become a real problem as of late, no thanks to Jasper the Jerk. For some reason, I can't stop thinking about him and his piercing eyes. They pop up in my dreams, those green irises full of lust and longing.

Ridiculous, I know. He's at least a decade older than me, has his own law firm, and is stupidly hot. Oh, and he's my stepbrother. Not that any of that is relevant. Jasper isn't lusting after me, and I have no right to lust after him. And I'm not. Sure, I may have had a few steamy fantasies when I closed my eyes these last few days, but I can't control my subconscious.

My stomach growls, reminding me I skipped lunch today. I let out an exasperated sigh and scoot my chair back from my desk. I'm not getting anywhere with this essay, and certainly not on an empty stomach.

Making my way downstairs, I hop across the cold, hardwood floor, not wanting my bare feet to freeze. I'm about to sneak into the kitchen when I notice the light in the dining room is on. Weird. I thought everyone had left for the afternoon.

Tiptoeing toward the direction of the light, I freeze in place when I see Jasper sitting at the table, paper spread around him while he furiously types away on his laptop.

What the heck is he doing here?

My palms start sweating, and my heart pounds out a staccato rhythm inside my chest. I'm in ratty old pajama shorts and a worn-out t-shirt that hangs down almost past my shorts. I threw my hair up into a messy bun hours ago, and I'm sure it looks like a bird's nest on top of my head after I tugged at the strands in frustration over my assignment.

I'm about to spin around and dash upstairs to leave Jasper alone when he looks up. His eyes meet mine, something dark flashing in those green depths. When he blinks, it's gone.

"Faye," he says, clearing his throat.

"Jasper," I reply, taking a few steps toward him. I can't help it. My body seems to be drawn to his, despite my best efforts to stay away. "What are you working on?" I ask, reaching for one of the loose papers scattered over the table.

"Put that down," he snaps as he grabs the paper from my hand.

I roll my eyes and stroll through the dining room and into the kitchen. After making myself a peanut butter and jelly sandwich and snagging a handful of chips, I find myself walking back to the dining room table.

Veer left! Avoid the dining room; my mind screams at me to no avail.

My feet rebel against my better judgment, carrying me forward until I plop down in the chair right next to Jasper's.

He startles, then scoots a few inches away from me and tilts his screen away.

"I don't have cooties," I tell him with another roll of my eyes.

"Noted," is all he says.

Why am I here? Clearly, Jasper is irritated with me. I suppose that was part of my plan, but there's something else. I feel lighter when I'm around him. And not just because I enjoy riling him up. It's just… him. His presence. It makes no sense, but that's what my stupid heart and body seem to think.

I crunch on a few chips, noting the tick in Jasper's jaw. Shoving a few more in my mouth, I chew loudly, even managing to get a few crumbs on his precious papers.

"Seriously?" he grumbles.

"I'm just having a snack. You want some? Wouldn't want you to get all hangry on me again," I say with a smirk. Jasper lifts his eyes from his computer screen, pinning me with a glare. "Suit yourself." I shrug and continue my obnoxious eating. I don't know what it is about him, but I like seeing Jasper all worked up.

"Do you have to eat it right here?" He sounds annoyed, but at the same time, he starts clearing off a little space for me to set my plate down.

"Nope," I tell him with a grin. "To be fair, you're technically in my house, so…" I trail off before taking a huge bite of my sandwich. Jasper stares at my mouth, and I make sure to puff out my cheeks as I chew.

I'm expecting him to glare or roll his eyes at me, but instead, he keeps staring at me. It's like he's hypnotized or something. I swear he's not even blinking. Swallowing hard, I lick some peanut butter from my top lip. Jasper tracks the movement, making butterflies dance in my lower belly.

Out of the corner of my eye, I see Jasper's hand slowly

move toward my face. He cups my cheek, and lightning bolts shoot down my spine, sizzling every nerve ending along the way. Is he about to kiss me? Am I about to let him?

Holy crap, holy crap, holy—

Jasper swipes his thumb over the corner of my lips, removing a big glob of jelly. My eyes widen, and I jerk my face out of his hand, absolutely mortified. To think I was about to… no. I can't go there. What the hell is wrong with me lately?

"Didn't want you to get your mess all over my case files," Jasper grunts. He stares at his thumb for half a second, then licks the raspberry jelly off. *Oh fuck*. Why is that so hot?

I sputter for a brief moment, then manage to collect myself enough to form words. "Maybe if I knew what you were working on, I'd respect it a little more."

"Somehow, I doubt it." His tone is irritated, but I see his lip twitching as if he's holding back a smile. I don't know if I'd survive an honest to god smile from Jasper.

"Try me."

Jasper looks at me out of the corner of his eye, and I bat my eyelashes. I might even pout, but only a little bit. I know I've won when he sighs and turns his computer toward me.

"My client is Winchester Mansfield," he starts. I snort out a laugh, and Jasper glances my way, one eyebrow lifted.

"Sorry, but that name sounds like it's a Downton Abbey extra," I say with a laugh.

He lets a grin slip through his otherwise aloof exterior. The sight of it warms me up, making my heart flutter and my lady parts clench. *Get it together, woman!*

"Yes, well, he's about as annoying as that show," Jasper retorts.

"What? You don't like Downton Abbey? What is wrong with you?"

"I haven't seen it."

"Then how do you know it's annoying?"

He clears his throat. "I know I don't like period pieces, and from what I can recollect, the show was mostly popular with women, so–"

"So you just assumed it was beneath you?" I push, just wanting to get a reaction. I don't really care what he thinks about the show. I didn't watch past season two if I'm honest.

"No, that's not what I was… look, how did we even get here? I thought you wanted to know about the case."

"I do," I say, inching my chair closer. Jasper glances at our chairs, which are now nearly touching. I don't know what I'm doing, only that I need to be closer to him. Jasper has this calming, steady way about him. He might be a little - okay, a lot - surly, but there's something so solid and dependable about him, too. I crave that. Someone to rely on. Someone to calm the storm.

"Fine. No more interruptions then."

"No promises."

Jasper coughs, but I swear I hear a little laugh in there. I hang on to it with everything in me. I find I like making Jasper smile. Almost as much as I enjoy making him roll his eyes at me.

He goes on to explain the property situation between his client and a neighboring family who wants to claim part of the client's land. I look at his computer screen as he shows me an aerial view of the properties in question.

"Wait, is that upstate? Near Cayuga Lake?" I lean forward in my seat so I can see the screen better.

"Yeah," he murmurs. I look up at him, not realizing I'm practically sitting in his lap. Our eyes stay locked for a moment too long, but then I break our connection, moving my chair further away. I'm not sure what just happened, only that it's dangerous.

"Um…" I stutter out, trying to stop my racing thoughts.

"I-Is your client's land bordering the lake?" I ask, finally remembering what we were talking about.

"Yes," he grits out, clearly back in Jasper the Jerk mode.

"You know, there are *selenicereus grandiflorus* around Cayuga Lake."

"What the hell is that?"

I grin, liking the feeling of knowing something Jasper doesn't. "In layman's terms, they are called Night-Blooming Cereus." He continues to stare at me with a blank face.

I roll my eyes and grab his laptop, typing the plant name into his search engine and hitting enter. I pull up a website featuring the gorgeous, rare blooms of the *selenicereus grandiflorus.*

Jasper studies the flower then glances at me, silently encouraging me to continue.

"These plants are pretty rare and often protected by wildlife restoration organizations." Jasper nods, still not making the connection. "They only bloom for one night of the year, and the blossoms smell like sweet vanilla." I smile, remembering the magical night I saw one bloom for myself. It was an extra credit assignment for one of my classes, one I was all too happy to do.

"Okay... well, thank you for that non-sequitur–"

"You're not listening!" I huff out. "Check your client's property, especially right by the edge of the lake. Weirdly enough, the Night-Blooming Cereus is a cactus, but it can be found growing in some odd places. If you find one, you can register the area as a preservation space, therefore prohibiting any construction that would disturb the area." I cross my arms over my chest and tip my chin up, practically preening at my knowledge.

Jasper stares at me, assessing me and picking me apart. His green eyes peer into mine like he's searching for something. Finally, he speaks. "How do you know that?"

"I'm a botanical science major," I tell him. His eyebrows shoot up his forehead, and I giggle. He looks cartoonish and silly, which are two words I never thought would describe Jasper. "Didn't think I had the brains, huh?" I meant for it to come out as teasing, but I think my insecurity bled through. No one thinks I'll make it as a scientist. My mom thinks it's silly for me to try.

"I didn't say that," Jasper finally answers. "You're smart enough to do whatever you want. And clever enough to get away with anything you set your mind to."

I gape at him, then blink rapidly, brushing away the sudden rush of emotions welling up in my eyes. "Um, thanks," I whisper, looking back down at my mostly empty plate. It's all too much. My head is spinning, and I'm not sure what to make of Jasper's words, let alone the way he's looking at me. "Glad to be of service," I say, shaking away the weird tension creeping up my spine.

"Faye..."

"I better get back to studying," I announce, standing up from my chair. "If I'm right about the flowers, you owe me a consultation fee," I tell him as I pick up my plate.

Jasper lets out a chuckle, making me ridiculously proud of myself. "And what will that be?"

I shrug and give him a smirk. "I guess we'll see." I *accidentally* tip my plate, letting the crumbs of my chips and sandwich fall onto a stack of papers. Jasper sighs dramatically, making me giggle.

"Brat," he grumbles. I peer at him over my shoulder as I walk into the kitchen, and I swear he's smiling.

I think I'm in trouble.

CHAPTER FIVE

JASPER

The words on my screen blur together, and I lean back in my chair, barely suppressing a yawn. Looking down at the files spread out on the desk and the hours-old coffee sitting off to the right, I decide it's time to pack up and call it a night. I'm not even sure why I came over here in the first place.

Okay, that's a lie. I know exactly why I'm at my dad and Monica's house, and it has nothing to do with either of them. It doesn't even have to do with the case, although that's the lame excuse I gave my old man when I asked if I could use his office to work on the Mansfield situation. I made up some BS about needing to borrow a book, and then I sat in his office and worked until both my dad and Monica went off to bed on the other side of this ridiculous mansion.

Some desperate part of me just wanted to be closer to Faye, to have the chance to glimpse her beautiful body and breathe in her sweet, floral scent. It's a dangerous game, but I can't seem to help myself. The woman has me under a goddamn spell.

I push the leather office chair back and stand up,

stretching out my sore muscles as another yawn escapes me. The decor here is dark, solid, and classic, much like my father. Every other inch of this place is decked out with portraits, expensive knick knacks, crystal vases, and the occasional jewel-encrusted frame. It's over the top and tacky, but then again, I'd expect nothing less from Monica.

Faye was in her room all evening, so my not-so-subtle plan was a bust. I haven't seen her since she cracked the case wide open a few days ago. Sure enough, I went stomping through the edge of the lake on Winchester's property and found what I think are the night-blooming-whatever-the-fuck plants. I sent some photos to one of my assistants to do more research, but I'm pretty confident about what I saw.

I roll the tension from my shoulders before gathering my files and shoving them into my briefcase, already fighting the urge to walk down the hall into Faye's room. I just need to see her face and make sure she's really in her bed. What if she snuck out? Oh, god, what if she's at some frat party?

The sound of paper tearing snaps me from my thoughts. I look down to see my fists are clenched so tightly I ripped some of my notes. I'm not jealous. I'm *not*. I'm concerned. Any older brother would be.

But I'm not her brother. I'm barely her stepbrother. We didn't grow up together. We barely know each other. I have no right to be this protective.

But the fire roaring through my chest says otherwise. Every goddamn muscle tenses with the need to be near Faye, to look into those amethyst eyes and find my absolution. I flex, feeling possessiveness ripple throughout my body, settling deep down in my bones. She's a part of me now.

Fuck.

Grabbing my jacket and briefcase, I head into the hall, flicking off the light on my way out. It's nearly one in the morning, and the entire house is dark, except for a few dim nightlights at the end of the hall and on the stairs. I wonder if Monica found them at Tiffany's.

I make my way past Faye's room, but then my feet lock into place, almost making me topple over. *What the hell?*

Staring down at my treacherous feet, I frown, willing them to move again. Instead, I turn toward the closed door, resting my hand on the knob. *Don't do this,* battles with, *it's just one peek,* making my head spin.

Before I get a chance to debate myself any further, a muffled cry sounds from the other side of the door. I don't hesitate to throw the damn thing wide open, adrenaline coursing through my veins as I go into beast mode, needing to eviscerate the threat.

I stand in the doorway, taking in the scene before me. Faye's room is cast in shadows, the only light coming from the hallway. My eyes barely have time to adjust before another gut-wrenching sob pierces the otherwise quiet darkness.

"Faye," I call out, rushing over to her side. I look down at the curvy pixie all tangled up in her sheets. Her head thrashes back and forth, and her lips tremble as she gasps for air.

I'm not sure what I'm doing, but I need to take her pain away. Kneeling on the bed, I reach out toward Faye, my hand hovering just over her shoulder. Gently, so gently, I grip her arm and shake, hoping to wake her from whatever nightmare she's living.

"Faye, wake up," I urge her. She shakes her head no, squeezing her eyes shut. "Come on, baby girl, it's just a dream. You're safe."

I try tucking some of her wild hair behind her ear, but she whimpers and jerks away from me, still fighting the demons in her head.

"No..." she cries, throwing an arm out to block some

imaginary threat.

Jesus, what is going on in her head? What happened to her? How often does she have these terrible dreams? And for how long? All answers I need as soon as possible.

The beautiful, broken woman takes in shallow breaths, her entire body trembling as I sit here, at a loss for what to do. Going on pure instinct, I gather Faye up into my arms, crushing her against my chest.

I'm expecting her to fight me, but Faye clings to me instead, burying her face into the side of my neck. "I've got you," I whisper, holding her in place with a hand on the back of her head. I gently stroke her back with my other hand, rocking us gently while she calms down. "You're safe," I tell her over and over.

Faye's tears wet my shirt and skin, and I absorb them, wanting to soak up every last bit of fear. I don't know how long we stay wrapped up in each other, but eventually, she tenses. Reluctantly, I pull back, though I still keep her close.

"J-Jasper?" Faye stutters out, her voice scratchy from crying.

"I'm right here," I assure her, brushing her hair out of her tear-stained face.

"Why... I mean, what...? Wh-what are..." Faye shivers as another round of tears pours down her cheeks. She looks so confused, so damn vulnerable and innocent at this moment. Purple eyes shine up at me, making my heart clench painfully.

I cup the side of her face, wiping stray tears away with my thumb. I have no words for this precious, complicated, frustrating, perfect woman. I can feel her heart beating against mine as she curls further into my chest.

"I've got you," I tell her again, pressing my lips to her forehead.

Finally, Faye relaxes, taking a deep breath as she melts

against me. I want to beat my chest in victory, knowing I could make my woman feel safe even when she's still struggling through whatever the fuck just happened.

"I'm sorry," she whispers. It's so soft, so broken, I almost don't hear it.

"There's nothing to apologize for, baby. I've got you." I don't know where these words are coming from, but they seem to be working. I wish I had more sweet things to say, but I've never been good at that shit. I vow to be better, softer, and more patient with Faye. I have no idea what this woman has been through, but she's mine now. No way in hell am I letting her go now that I know what it feels like to have her in my arms.

Faye takes a deep breath then untangles herself from me. I don't like it. I want her right back here, where she belongs. Doesn't she feel it, too?

"Um, I..." Faye starts as she grips one of the sheets that fell off. She covers herself with the thin blanket, and I suddenly notice she's wearing nothing but a tank top and booty shorts.

Not the fucking time to be a perv, I scold myself.

"Thanks for... well, thanks," she stutters out.

"What happened? Do you get nightmares often?"

Faye tenses then scoots further away from me. I hate it. Doesn't she know she needs be by my side?

"I, well, I used to. When I was little... never mind."

"Tell me," I encourage her, gathering her other blankets and urging her to lay down.

Faye's eyes track my every movement as I cover her up, tucking the blanket into her sides so she feels safe and secure.

"Thank you," she murmurs, blinking slowly. She nibbles on her bottom lip, and I almost break. I almost lean forward and close the distance between us, tasting her sweet lips and salty tears. "I think... I think you should probably go."

I jolt back, her words stinging as if she slapped me. Go? *Go?* I can't leave her. Not in this state. Looking down at Faye, all wrapped up in blankets, tears still drying on her rounded cheeks, I want nothing more than to curl myself around her and rock her to sleep. However, I can tell she needs space. I may have just realized she's mine, but Faye doesn't know that yet. She's certainly not ready to have that conversation in this state of mind, either.

Reluctantly, I nod my head and stand up. "Are you alright?"

Faye doesn't say anything for a moment, but the half-hearted smile she gives me speaks volumes. "I will be."

Those three words hit me in the gut. How long has my woman lived with whatever terrorizes her? Does anyone else know? Do they care? Thinking back on everything I've learned about Monica, I know she's never once comforted her daughter after a nightmare. My heart breaks all over again for my sweet girl.

When I can't stand to be in the room another minute without pulling Faye back into my arms, I slowly turn around and stalk back out into the hallway. I give her one last look over my shoulder, then close the door.

Each step away from Faye is more painful than the last, but I need to leave. She's obviously been traumatized, and she doesn't trust me enough to talk about it. Fuck, that hurts, but I can't blame her. I also can't leave her like this.

Instead of walking out to my car and driving home like I should, I grab a blanket and pillow off the couch in my dad's office. I set up camp right outside of Faye's door, hunkering down for a terrible night's sleep.

My neck aches, my back is sore, and my chest feels hollow, but there's nowhere else I'd rather be. Protecting Faye is my new mission in life.

CHAPTER SIX

FAYE

"That's so freaking adorable!" I tell my bestie, Sarah, via FaceTime.

"I know! Dylan is secretly a big old teddy bear," she says with a dreamy smile.

Sarah and her man, Dylan, have been deliriously in love for the last few weeks. I'm thrilled for my friend, of course. She deserves someone who will love her sassiness as much as her brilliant mind. Things started out a bit rocky for Dylan and Sarah, what with him being her older professor and all, but when push came to shove, these two chose each other over every obstacle.

"I'm so happy things are going well with you and Dylan," I tell her, giving her my best smile. I shove down the jealous thought trying to rear its ugly head. I can't think about Jasper or how I secretly wish we could have a happily ever after. Especially after last night.

"How are things going with Jasper?"

I jerk my head up, my eyes going wide at Sarah's question. Did I say something out loud? Is my stupid crush written all over my face?

"Jasper?" I croak out.

"Yeah... Jasper the Jerk, I believe we've dubbed him. Everything okay?"

"Yes. Absolutely. Of course. Why wouldn't it be?"

Sarah narrows her eyes, giving me *the look*. She knows I'm full of it. "Okay, how about the truth this time? Do I need to talk to him? Or have Dylan knock some sense into him? He can't treat you like crap, especially in your own home!" I love my bestie. She's loyal and kind-hearted, and I know she'll always have my back.

"He's not... It's not..." I sigh, adjusting the pillows on my bed so I can settle in more comfortably. This might be a long catch-up sesh. "We sort of... had a moment," I hedge.

"You kissed?! Oh, my god, why didn't you call me the second your lips left his?"

"Sarah!" I hiss, turning the volume down on my phone in case anyone is listening in. "No, we didn't kiss. God!" She just giggles, which makes me smile and roll my eyes. "So dramatic," I tease, knowing I'm way more dramatic than Sarah.

"So, what happened then?"

"Last night, I had one of my nightmares again," I say quietly.

Sarah's eyes soften, nearly making me cry. She knows all about my bad dreams. She's even witnessed a few during our sleepovers growing up. "Faye, I'm so sorry. I didn't know you still got them."

I shrug, trying to brush off her concern, but Sarah knows me better than that. "They aren't as frequent, but when I'm stressed or feeling out of control, I'm right back there, trapped in the darkness." My friend nods, encouraging me to continue. "Anyway, Jasper was here for some reason. I think he came over to work in his dad's office or something. All I know is that I was being suffocated by the empty darkness one minute, and the next minute, Jasper was holding me."

"Really?" Sarah gasps. She looks at me with all the lovey-dovey hope she's been carrying around ever since finding her soulmate. "That's so sweet."

I snort out a laugh. "Jasper isn't sweet."

"Are you sure? Waking you up from a nightmare and holding you sounds pretty darn swoon-worthy to me."

"He's not... he's... look, he's *Jasper*," I say, emphasizing his name. Truthfully, I've missed his touch. I woke up this morning half hoping he'd be in bed with me, but I know I'm being clingy and crazy. "Anyway, he's my stepbrother, so this conversation is officially over."

It's Sarah's turn to laugh. "You know that's never the case with us," she says with a teasing lilt to her voice. "Besides, who says forbidden love can't work out? Look at me!"

I smile at my bestie, happy that she's happy. Things aren't so cut and dried for me. Yes, she got her man and her fairy-tale ending, but that doesn't mean I should rush into anything head first.

I'm about to tell her just that when my door swings open.

"Faye! There you are," my mom snaps as she steps into my room. "What are you doing? What are you wearing? Shouldn't you be getting ready for your date tonight?"

I groan and give Sarah a pouty face before waving good-bye. She knows that when Hurricane Monica blows in, there's nothing to do but wait out the storm.

"The date is canceled," I tell her flatly.

"Canceled?" The alarm in her voice doesn't fit the situation, but then again, that's par for the course with my mother. "He canceled, or you canceled?"

"Does it matter?"

"Yes! God, Faye, I've done everything I can to give you a good life, and all I'm asking is that you follow suit. You want to afford a home and a car and the nice things I've been able to provide for us, don't you?"

"Jobs in the scientific field pay well, depending on the area of specialty," I retort.

She huffs out a breath like I knew she would. "Science." She mutters the word like a curse, then rubs her temples, looking every bit the exasperated socialite housewife. "I'm talking about wealth, Faye. Real money. The way to get it in this world is to play the game."

"No, mom. That's how *you* get it."

"Not anymore," she mutters. "I'm not as young as I once was. Not as flexible, either."

I grimace at her tactlessness, trying to erase the image of my mother being *flexible*. "Is that why you're with Conner?" I regret the question as soon as it slips out of my mouth.

My mother's eyes snap to mine, the crease in her forehead a warning for me to quit while I'm ahead. When I don't respond, she smirks. "Conner is a decent man. Reliable. It's unbecoming for a mature woman to be without a husband. Besides, I want to settle down. Once Conner retires from the firm, we'll be able to live quite comfortably."

"Mmhm," I say with a nod, though I know what she really means.

My mother tried marrying another millionaire, but she found she was past her prime. The rich, shallow assholes she usually goes for all wanted younger women, leaving poor, gold-digging Monica Charmichael to slum it with the *very* wealthy instead of the *obscenely* wealthy.

"Anyway, this isn't about my future. It's about yours."

"Right," I mutter under my breath.

"You'll call Nigel and reschedule your date, Faye."

"No, thank you. Pass." I scroll through my phone, trying to ignore my mother's demands.

She grabs my phone out of my hands and glares at me. "You will not be rude to the Sullivans. They're a very well-connected family, and last month, Nigel noticed you at that benefit concert. Amazing, really, since you were wearing the red dress that shows off your wide hips and rolls. I hate that dress. Why do you still have it?"

Because you hate it, I want to yell. I don't because I've learned to pick my battles.

"No matter," my mother continues, tossing my phone on the foot of my bed before opening my closet. She proceeds to go through my wardrobe, muttering to herself about putting me on a diet until my dress size is in the single digits.

I sit up in bed, staring out my window, trying to ignore the jabs my mom keeps sending my way. Flabby arms, thick thighs, and a bit of a belly that I could get rid of if I went carb-free for a year. Not going to happen.

My mom rushes around my room then calls the salon, making an appointment for me tomorrow afternoon. "The full works," she confirms over the phone. "Yes, for my daughter, Faye. She's..." Mother looks at me over her shoulder, her judgy eyes flitting from head to toe. "She'll take some time. Hair, makeup, waxing, plucking, and whatever else you can do to help."

I roll my eyes but turn around so she can't see how her words affect me. I don't care what my mom thinks. At least, that's what I tell myself. But when all I hear from her is how I'm too big, too loud, too annoying, too... *me*, it still hurts.

A few minutes later, the commotion is over. I look behind me, where my mom has set out a slinky silver dress and sky-high heels, red bottoms, of course. "I'll call the Sullivans and explain you were under the weather tonight but are looking forward to seeing Nigel tomorrow evening."

"Mother, I don't–"

"Just one date," she sighs. "God, Faye, I'm doing all the work here. You just have to show up and flirt a little. Just try for me, please? After everything I've sacrificed for you? After everything your *father* sacrificed for you to live a good life?"

I inhale sharply at the reminder of my dad. He made the ultimate sacrifice; his life for mine. I'm pissed when I feel tears stinging my eyes and clogging my throat. She knows I'm powerless to argue with her when she brings out that defense.

"That's what I thought. Get your beauty rest, dear daughter. You need to put on the show of a lifetime tomorrow night."

I refuse to look up until she's gone. I won't let her see my tears.

Standing, I start pacing around my room, frustrated, trapped, and helpless. I'm stuck in a life I didn't ask for. I keep holding out for graduation, for a taste of true freedom and the opportunity to forge my own path. Every day here in this house chips away at that hope. I desperately want to make my own way in life, no strings attached. My secret? I don't think I'm cut out for it.

I dig my fingers into a throw pillow on my bed, clenching my fists and trying to rip the damn thing in half. Restless energy swirls in my chest, pulsing outward and pushing me to do something with this pent-up anger.

I want to trash this room. I want to rip the mirrors off the walls and watch them shatter around me. I want to throw my clothes in a pile on the floor and run them over with a lawnmower. I want to scratch and claw and roar out my anger, but I know it's pointless. No one cares.

Taking a cleansing breath, I try to stop myself from trembling. When I'm all worked up like this, there's only one place I feel safe.

Grabbing my phone and my jacket, I tiptoe down the stairs and out the back door. A cool breeze tangles in my hair, whipping it around my face. I tighten my jacket around my shoulders and follow the well-worn path to my special hiding spot.

Pulling back the long, slender branches of the willow tree on the far east side of the property, I slip inside my beautiful rose garden. The sweet, perfumed scent of wild roses, beach roses, and French roses wash over me, and I close my eyes, inhaling deeply.

My little garden is tucked away in a forgotten corner of the estate. It's fenced in on three sides, with a huge weeping willow tree acting as a curtain of sorts to hide my precious roses from prying, unappreciative eyes.

I walk slowly around the space, checking on my babies. The wild roses are always going strong, so much so I often need to trim them back. I had some difficulty getting the French roses to blossom this year, but once I added a few coffee grounds to balance the acidity in the soil, I couldn't stop the thing from blooming. And then there's my new addition to the collection. The Damask rose. Right now, the buds are still coiled tightly together, but I know in a few weeks, the gorgeous, light peach petals will unfold in a swirling pattern. I smile just thinking about how beautiful it will be. It's good to have things to look forward to, even if it's all your own magic.

After visiting the different plots of rose bushes, I sit down in the middle of my garden on a patch of soft grass. This is my happy place. My peaceful place. My sanctuary. Closing my eyes, I lay back on the grass, letting the earth cradle me.

A rustling noise catches my attention, and I snap my eyes open. I've run into a bunny or two out here, but nothing too big or scary. That sound was more than just a small critter, however. I look around the plot of land, waiting to hear the sound again.

This time, I notice the weeping willow branches swaying slightly, and I follow the movement until my eyes land on two large shoes sticking out from the bottom of a wild rose bush. I suppress a grin as I drag my eyes up, up, up, giggling when I see Jasper trying to hide behind a bush. His wide shoulders aren't even a little bit hidden, and his elbows poke out on either side of the bush.

I should be angry that he's here, invading my private sanctuary. Instead, I feel… relieved. Like I can breathe for the first time since my mom came bursting into my room.

"I think I know why you became a lawyer," I call out as I stand up, putting my hands on my hips.

The rose bush shakes, and Jasper lets out a string of curses before finally stepping out into the open. His hair has a few leaves in it, and his expensive suit is covered in dirt and little sticks. It's pretty endearing, and I find myself smiling as he brushes off his clothes.

"Uh, why's that?" Jasper asks, rubbing the back of his neck.

Oh, my god, are his ears red? Is he blushing? Wow, it's not fair how adorable that is. "Because you're a terrible criminal," I say flatly.

Jasper doesn't even try to hide his grin, and holy crap, he's *dazzling*. "I was just… checking up on you," he says, looking around at the roses and grass, and pretty much everywhere except me. I like seeing him flustered.

"I'm okay. And about last night–"

Jasper puts his hand up, palm out. "I was checking in on you then, too."

I nod, assessing him as he walks closer to me. "Well, here I am," I breathe out, tipping my head back to look up at him. He's so close, I can feel the warmth of his body and smell his clean peppermint scent.

"Here you are," he murmurs. "My beautiful pixie in her rose garden."

His words are so soft, I'm not sure I was meant to hear them. Did he call me *his*?

Jasper leans down, closer, closer, closer until his mouth

hovers over mine. His breath teases my lips as I stare into his green eyes. *Fall* into them. They hold such depth, a touch of darkness, but also overwhelming tenderness. For me?

My eyes flutter closed, and I lift up on my tiptoes, craving this, needing this, wanting to be pressed against him from head to toe.

"Faye..." the low, growled sound makes me whimper. He sounds like he's in pain from holding back. I don't want him to. Not anymore.

"Jasp–"

His phone rings, and we spring apart as if caught in the act. Shit, I guess we almost were. Right? What exactly were we doing? Does this mean anything to him?

Jasper gives me a pained look then pulls his phone out of his pocket. I nod my head and spin around, tending to another rose bush. My heart is hammering in my ears, my blood pumping as the adrenaline slowly disperses.

When I turn around, Jasper is gone.

CHAPTER SEVEN

JASPER

"Another late night, son?" my dad asks as he walks past the dining room where I'm sitting and into the kitchen.

"Uh, yeah, hopefully, we'll be settling this case soon," I say, concentrating on my screen so I don't have to look him in the eye.

I'm not a fan of lying to my father, but what choice do I have? I can't very well tell him I overheard Monica sending Faye off on a date, and I got so jealous I nearly passed out from the rush of blood. I definitely can't tell him I borrowed Faye's phone while she was getting ready for the evening and got her info, as well as turned on location tracking. It's probably best he doesn't know I've been staring at my phone, watching, waiting, willing the little dot to start moving again, so I know Faye's on her way home to me.

"Good, good," my dad says. "Let me know if you need a second pair of eyes on anything. Or if you need to borrow another book." The way he says it makes me think he's on to me, but when I look up, my father is already on his way back upstairs. He and Monica live on the east side of the mansion, leaving Faye to her own devices on the west side. I can't say I mind, especially since I don't know what the fuck I'm going to do when Faye comes home.

Looking at my phone for the six hundredth time this evening, I grit my teeth when I see it's just past nine-thirty. Faye left around seven. It doesn't take two and a half hours to eat. Why isn't she back yet?

Just as I start to consider driving to the restaurant and picking Faye up myself, my phone dings, letting me know Faye is on the move. I clutch the device in my hand, staring at the dot slowly coming back into the neighborhood. Thank fucking god. It wouldn't have ended well if I showed up to get Faye myself.

Satisfied that Faye will be here soon, I flip through some papers and pretend to look busy. I refuse to keep looking at my phone or I'll go completely crazy counting the seconds until her car pulls up.

Instead, I anxiously await her arrival, not knowing what to say or what to do. I have to make her understand. She's mine, which means she can't go out on any more dates. I overheard how unhappy Faye was with this setup, but it sounded like she just had to sit there and eat dinner. It still took every last ounce of strength in me not to throw Faye over my shoulder and load her up into my car before driving her far away from here. Soon, but not right now. I need to figure out the best way to claim her without causing an upheaval in our lives. Though, honestly, I'm beginning to care less and less about propriety at this point.

I need her. It's as simple and as complicated as that.

I need Faye's mischievous smile and bright purple eyes. I need her tinkling laughter and soft blush. I need her full lips, her sinful curves, her breathy moans as I sink into her for the first time.

Fuck.

A car door slams, jarring me from my fantasies. High heels click against the walkway, then the side door swings open, bouncing off the wall with a loud bang. Faye has arrived, ladies and gentlemen.

I make a point to jot down notes on my yellow legal pad, looking studious and not suspicious at all. I hope.

Faye lets out a sigh, and though I can't see her from where I'm sitting in the dining room, I can feel the weariness down to my very soul. I'm about to go to her and wrap my arms around my sweet girl and demand she tells me everything on her mind, but Monica gets to her first.

"Faye? Is that you?" she screeches from somewhere upstairs. Faye groans softly, making me smirk. I think she likes her mom about as much as I do. "Stay right there. I need a full report."

I ball up my fists, then let out a slow breath. I don't want to hear the details of Faye's date, even if she hated it. I don't like thinking about her with anyone else but me. Listening to Faye slip her shoes off and grab a glass of water from the next room, I consider when the best time is to inform her she's mine.

"Faye," Monica says once she's clambered down the stairs. "Good lord, child, why is your hair such a mess? And your makeup…"

I growl at Monica's insult. She never has a nice word to say about anyone, especially her own daughter. That will change soon if she wants to stay in Faye's life.

"I'm fine, thanks," Faye says sarcastically.

"Of course, you are. Why wouldn't you be?"

I hear a strangled out growl and realize it's coming from Faye. "Why wouldn't I be fine? Oh, I don't know. Maybe because you set me up on a date with a guy ready for retirement?" she yells. "Or how about the fact that he took several little blue pills and then decided it was my obligation to help him work them off?"

What the fuck?

I stand up, knocking the dining room chair to the floor. Cracking my neck and rolling my shoulders, I try to push away the red clouding my vision. Some old motherfucking creep took Viagra and then tried to make a move on Faye? No. No fucking way.

"Oh, please. Nigel is harmless," Monica says dismissively. "I mean, he didn't really do anything. Right?" Her voice wavers for a split second, allowing a shred of humanity to peek through Monica's otherwise impenetrable armor.

I will never forgive her for putting her daughter in danger.

I step into the kitchen, needing to have my eyes on Faye and make sure she's unharmed. Her back is facing me, and I watch her put her hands on her hips and square off with her mother.

"Fuck you!" she screams. "How did you become so callous? So money-driven? And why do you expect me to be the same way?"

I keep my distance, wanting Faye to have her moment. Monica deserves so much worse than Faye's words and judgments, but it's a start.

"You think you're better than me, dear daughter? You're not. You're naive to how the world works, but you've got to toughen up."

"Toughen up? Are you serious? What happened to you, Mom? You and dad were so in love–"

"Ha," Monica laughs hollowly. "And look how that turned out. One dead husband and one ungrateful daughter. Love is a weakness, but wealth makes you stronger."

Faye gasps, and I start walking toward her, needing to hold her, touch her, do *something* to show her I'm here.

"You don't mean that," Faye counters, her voice cracking.

"I do. I only wish I'd figured it out sooner. Then I wouldn't have to deal with..." Monica trails off, letting the implication hang in the air. Her eyes snap to mine, and she startles, noticing me for the first time. Then, she sets her jaw and hardens her eyes, digging in and standing her ground.

I'm right behind Faye and rest my hand on her shoulder. She jerks away from me, twisting her head to look in my direction. "Faye–"

"No!" she yells, backing away from both her mother and me. "I can't... I can't... I can't deal with this anymore. I..." Faye coughs and chokes on a sob, propelling me forward. I fucking need to hold her, need to be near her so I can take on her pain like I did during her nightmare.

She looks at her mom, then at me, before spinning on her heel and sprinting upstairs.

"Faye!" I call out, taking off after her.

"Leave her be. She's always so dramatic," Monica says.

I grunt, ignoring the insufferable woman, and take the stairs two at a time to catch up with Faye. I reach the top just in time to see Faye slam her door shut. Pulling air into my lungs, I pause outside her room, needing to keep myself in check. I can deal with Monica later, and I *will* be dealing with her. Right now, I need to hold my broken little pixie and make sure no one harmed a hair on her head.

A loud crash sounds from the other side of the door, followed by glass breaking. I shove the door open, stunned at what I find. Faye launches what appears to be a music box into a hanging picture of her and her mother, causing both to break and fall to the floor, joining another shattered frame.

Tears stream down her face as she heaves out uneven breaths. My girl is shaking with rage, sorrow, and frustration. I can see it, fucking feel it with each rapid beat of her heart. Faye is trapped, caged in, and struggling to keep her head above water. It's all too much for her to carry, but she's not alone anymore.

I lean against the door frame, allowing Faye's wild, pent-up fury to escape. As long as she's not hurting herself, I think she needs this release.

Faye tears through her closet, ripping dresses and tossing shoes into the wall. She swipes everything off of her vanity, watching as nail polish and eyeshadow spill onto the carpet. She stares at herself in the cracked mirror, her breathing ragged and her muscles tense. The feral look in her eyes dims, leaving fresh tears in its place.

She collapses onto the ground, and I rush over to her, kneeling and scooping her up into my arms. Faye tries to wiggle out of my embrace, but I pick her up and cradle her against my chest, making my way over to her bed. I check for any glass or sharp objects before laying her down and crawling in next to her. I pull her against me so we're facing each other, then wrap her up in my arms.

"What are you doing?" Faye asks through sniffles.

"Holding you," I answer, nuzzling into the top of her head. Her silky black hair tickles my skin, the smell of roses permeating every cell. She's still half-heartedly trying to escape, but I can tell she just wants me to hold her tighter. So, I do, grinning when she stops squirming and relaxes against me.

"Why?" she whispers, snuggling closer.

"Because I need it. You need it, too, don't you?" Faye doesn't say anything. She just nods. I press a kiss to her forehead, closing my eyes and inhaling her sweet scent. "I've got you, baby girl," I murmur. "I'm right here."

"I'm not like my mother," she says softly. "I didn't ask for any of this, and I don't want to follow in her footsteps." Her tone is low, and her voice is so quiet I almost don't hear her.

"I know," I assure her, her words piercing me to my core. I

made assumptions about my Faye, and I know it hurt her. I feel like an idiot, but I'll just have to spend the rest of my life making it up to her. "What happened tonight?" I ask.

Faye sighs and adjusts so we're as close as possible. "Just an old, entitled asshole who thinks money will make everything go away."

The way she says it makes me think this isn't the first time Monica put her in this position. I hate it. Never again. "Did he touch you?" I growl.

Faye rolls her eyes, but I don't even blink. I need to know.

"He tried, but I put him in his place. Kicked him in his saggy old balls and booked it out of the restaurant." She smirks, and an odd mix of pride and rage churn in my gut. I'm proud of her for standing up for herself, but Jesus, the thought of someone else's hands on her, without her permission... "Hey," she whispers. "I'm okay."

I squeeze my eyes shut, willing the anger to fade into the background. I hold my precious girl for long moments, whispering that she's safe with me. Faye's tears eventually dry, and she looks up at me, the faintest spark of hope in her violet eyes. Cupping her cheek, I brush a few strands of hair away from her face. I stare at her trembling lips, then focus on her brilliant eyes, framed in dark lashes.

"What's happening?" she whispers.

I feel more than hear her words as they skate across my skin. "I'm showing you who you belong to," I say before pressing my lips to hers.

Her taste hits my tongue, and I'm immediately addicted. Faye moans so softly, so sweetly, I can't help but growl like the beast I've become. Her fist tightens around my shirt where she's been clinging to me, and she pulls me closer, trying to feel all of me. Shit, I want that, too.

My hand slides from her cheek to the back of her head, and I tangle my fingers in her silky hair, holding my sweet girl in place while I claim her with my mouth. Slipping my tongue past her swollen lips, I lick the roof of her mouth, grunting in satisfaction when she shivers.

My other hand traces Faye's curves, her breasts, the slight dip in her waist, and her wide, mouthwatering hips. I grip her thigh, lifting slightly so I can shove my leg between hers. Faye instinctively grinds down on me, the heat of her pussy rubbing against my pant leg.

"Faye," I groan, breaking our kiss so I can trail my lips down her throat. I nip at her sensitive flesh, then lick away the sting. Jesus, I want more. More of her flavor, more of her surrendering sighs, more, more, *more*.

I flip Faye on her back and hover over her, resting my weight with a hand on either side of her head. She blinks her eyes open, a sweet blush spreading over her cheeks and neck. She smiles shyly then reaches out and runs her fingers through my hair. I close my eyes, savoring her touch.

Faye surprises me by digging her fingernails into the back of my head and pulling me down on top of her. My shock doesn't last for long. Gathering up her wrists, I pin them above her, then dip my head down to nibble and suck her neck.

I chuckle as she writhes beneath me, then put an end to both our misery and kiss her, full and deep. Faye rolls her hips and clutches my hand that's pinning her wrists down. She spreads her legs beneath me, cradling my hips between her thighs. I growl as I thrust my raging dick against her core, spurting precum when I feel how fucking hot and wet she is.

"God, Jasper…" she whimpers, crossing her ankles behind my back.

Jesus, I want to rip off our clothes and sink into her pussy over and over, fucking her into the mattress until she shouts my name and creams all over my cock.

But not here. Not like this.

I give my sexy little vixen one last drugging kiss, then roll over, adjusting Faye so she's stretched out over my chest. We're both breathing heavily, and Faye tucks her face into the side of my neck. I comb my fingers through her hair, then let them trail down her back before reversing my path. Each gentle stroke calms her down more and more, and it brings me unreasonable satisfaction that Faye trusts me in this vulnerable state.

I know we have a lot to talk about when the morning comes, but for now, I'm content to stay wrapped up in my Faye, protecting her from the whole damn world.

CHAPTER EIGHT

FAYE

I blink my eyes open, slowly becoming aware of warmth surrounding me. I can't remember the last time I slept so soundly, which is crazy, considering that date was a nightmare.

Then I remember.

Jasper.

As if on cue, arms circle my waist, pulling me closer. A crisp peppermint and pine scent fills my lungs, and I relax into Jasper's embrace, sighing when he presses a kiss to the back of my neck.

"Morning, baby girl," he rasps, nuzzling into my shoulder. His stubble scratches my skin, sparking a different kind of heat in my core.

"Morning," I whisper, clenching my thighs together.

God, I love when he calls me baby girl. Or sweetheart. Or anything, really. I crave his attention, his words, his hands on every inch of me. My hips move on their own, and I grind down on Jasper, gasping when I feel his hard length press against my ass.

"Fuck, sweetheart," he groans. "You're killing me here."

I look at him over my shoulder and smirk. "And look, I'm not even behind the wheel of my car," I tease.

Jasper narrows his beautiful green eyes at me, the corner of his lips curling up into the sexiest grin. He leans forward, nipping my shoulder, my neck, my chin, and finally, my lips. I giggle and try to escape the onslaught of love bites and kisses, but Jasper holds me close and tortures me with his lips and teeth.

"So sassy, even in the morning," he murmurs before kissing me fully.

His lips connect with mine as kiss after kiss keeps crashing into me like a bombardment of waves, each one more potent and devastating than the last. My body responds to him in a desperate and needy way. Before I even know what I'm doing, I turn in his embrace and climb over him, straddling his lap. Jasper's hands run up my thighs and grip my hips, rocking my body into his.

"Shit, baby girl," he groans as he kisses down my neck.

I love the feeling of his lips on my skin, how they softly tickle all the sensitive spots along my jaw, my neck, my shoulder. I shudder when his tongue darts out, warm and wet, sliding across my skin and setting it on fire.

"Please, Jasper, please..." I moan.

"Please, what?"

"I don't know. I want to feel more."

Jasper groans again and kisses me deeply as he slides his hands under the hem of my shirt. I feel the rough pads of his fingers dance over the skin on my lower back as I continue to rock into his hardness beneath me. He reaches lower, slipping his hands into the waistband of my sleep shorts. I got up in the middle of the night to change out of my sequined nightmare of a dress and didn't bother putting on a bra or panties. Jasper's ragged breath lets me know he doesn't mind. He grips my cheeks and lifts me easily, rubbing my body against his and angling me so his jean-clad cock hits my clit with each rocking motion.

I cry out, the ache only growing stronger. It's not enough to satisfy, the contact keeping me just on the edge. I feel like I'm reaching for something, my back arching, my muscles tensing, but I'm not quite there.

"More, please, I need more," I moan.

"Jesus, you're so fucking sexy. I'm trying to go slow here, baby."

"I don't want slow. I just want you."

This triggers something inside of Jasper. He growls, and I suddenly find my back pressed against the mattress as Jasper kneels between my legs.

"So beautiful," he whispers. His words are so quiet I'm not sure if they are meant for him or me.

Jasper hooks his thumbs in the waistband of my shorts and starts to tug them down. I squirm in anticipation, knowing I'm ready for whatever he's going to do next. I just need to feel him, need him to quench this fire burning deep inside.

"This okay, Faye?" His eyes search mine for permission, for any sign of hesitation.

"Yes, I need you, please," I pant.

I watch in fascination as Jasper's eyes flash darkly. His jaw tenses. His nostrils flare. He looks like a wild animal, and I find that I want to be his prey. I'm not scared of him; I don't think I could be. I trust Jasper completely, with all of me.

Jasper drags my clothes off of my body, slowly, so slowly, revealing inch after inch of skin. When he finally pulls everything off, his hands ghost up my legs, sending sparks across my skin and straight to my clit. His hands spread my legs wide, and I'm completely open before him.

I should feel embarrassed or shy, but the way he's staring at my center fills me with confidence and a strange kind of pride. Jasper massages the insides of my thighs, slowly working his way up to my dripping wet pussy. By the time he reaches my glistening folds, I'm shaking with pent-up energy and tension.

"Please," I whimper.

He swipes two fingers up my slit, gathering my cream and spreading it up around my clit. I buck my hips and feel more wetness leak out of me.

"Your juicy cunt is begging to be licked, isn't it?" My pussy contracts at his dirty words, my clit throbbing for his attention, for more of his words. "You like that, baby girl? Like when I talk dirty to you?" He keeps stroking me steadily, his fingers moving up and down the same path from my entrance to my clit and back again.

"Apparently," I manage to say, my voice breathy and cracking.

Jasper growls and leans down, placing a soft kiss on my mound of curls before inhaling my scent. Again, I should feel exposed or shy about what he's doing to me, but my body craves it. Those primal desires block out any other rational thought.

He scoots down and grips my right thigh, spreading me wider for him. Leaning down, he pauses with his face inches from my pussy. I buck my hips, needing to feel him. He chuckles, the sound vibrating through my body seconds before his tongue hits me for the first time.

He licks me in one long stroke, causing me to cry out. His hands slide under my ass, and he pulls me closer to him as he feasts on me. It's like the first taste sent him into a frenzy. I feel his mouth everywhere, seemingly all at once. He's lapping at me, batting my clit around, dipping his tongue inside of my tight hole, sucking my folds, and then starting all over again.

"Oh, god, Jasper, I... oh, god..." I can't form thoughts. I can only feel.

He growls into my pussy, sending jolts of electricity throughout my body as I grow impossibly wetter. Jasper lifts his head, panting for breath. I see my cream on his lips, his stubble, even his nose. It turns me on even more, though I can't explain why. He looks feral. Possessed. And then he grins wickedly and dives back in.

I'm trembling, tensing, teetering on the edge, the sweet torture calling me to give in to ultimate pleasure. IJasper-sucks my clit into his mouth and I fall off the cliff, crying out my release. I'm reduced to a violent, throbbing heartbeat.

I'm aware of Jasper crawling next to me and holding me in his arms. When the haze finally settles, Jasper is placing sweet kisses all over my face, my jaw, my neck, telling me how beautiful I am, how special, how sexy he finds me.

"You're so amazing, Faye. Fucking love watching you come, love giving you that pleasure."

"Mmm, I love it, too," I manage to say once I finally catch my breath.

"Oh, yeah?"

I look up at him and blush at his sexy smirk. "Mmhm," I smile.

"Good. I plan on devouring your sweet pussy every chance I get. I'm addicted to you, baby girl. In every way imaginable. I don't think I'll ever get enough of your taste, your scent, your sexy little moans. Fuck, Faye, just... goddamn."

I bite my lips to stifle a moan at his words. They are equal parts sexy and sweet, and I love both sides of Jasper.

After a few more minutes of snuggling, I lift my head, giving Jasper a devious look. He raises an eyebrow, watching me get off the bed as I stand in front of him. I reach out for him, and he immediately stands up, joining me.

"What's this about?" he whispers into the shell of my ear.

Instead of answering him with words, I wrap my arms around his neck and draw him in for a kiss. He parts his lips, letting me command this kiss and show him how much I want to please him, too. Jasper groans in frustration when I break our kiss but quickly changes his tune when I slide my hands down his chest and get on my knees for him.

"God, Faye…" he whispers, more to himself than to me.

I slip my hands under his t-shirt and run my fingers over his sculpted torso, grinning to myself when I feel him shudder. I love being in control of this massive man's body. It's a powerful, heady feeling to know my touch makes him crazy. Almost as crazy as his touch makes me.

His abs flex under my hands as they slide lower, lower, lower, dipping my fingers under the waistband of his pants. He groans, cursing under his breath as I reach inside and pull out his huge cock.

Jasper sucks in a breath and clenches his jaw as I grip him in my hand. I marvel at the soft, smooth skin and the way he grows even harder right before my eyes. My gaze wanders down to his balls, and not surprisingly, they are huge as well. Huge and heavy and apparently very sensitive, seeing as Jasper throws his head back and gasps for air when I cup them and massage them gently.

"Holy hell, Faye. Keep touching me like that, baby girl."

I lean forward, positioning myself so my lips are mere inches from the head of his shaft. "What if I lick you, too?" I whisper, blowing warm air over his cock and watching as a drop of precum forms and falls down his length.

"Fuck, yes, do that, god, please do that."

My tongue darts out and licks up the now steady stream of precum leaking out of him. One taste and I'm addicted. I don't know anything about giving a blow job, and what limited things I've heard about it gave me the impression that girls don't really like doing this. I have a feeling I will like it very much.

His salty, earthy taste explodes on my tongue, and I can't stop the moan that escapes my mouth. I continue to lick him like a lollipop and gently tug his balls. When he tangles his fingers in my hair, I know exactly what he's asking for, exactly what he needs.

I open my mouth and slowly slide down his throbbing dick. I have to practically pop my jaw out of place and stretch my lips farther than I thought possible to fit even part of him into my mouth. It's worth it to hear his sounds of pleasure and feel his hand tighten into a fist in my hair.

I love it. Love sucking on him, owning him, commanding him with the tip of my tongue. I love listening to his grunts and groans and figuring out what he likes and how I can give him more of it.

Jasper slips his other hand in my hair as well, massaging my scalp as I bob up and down. "Jesus, you feel so good. So fucking good."

I moan around him, soaking up his praise. Jasper snaps his hips, shoving his dick deeper into my mouth, the head of his shaft hitting the back of my throat and making me gag around his girth.

"Shit, sorry, baby. I'm having a hard time controlling myself with your sexy as fuck mouth wrapped around me."

I pull off of him with a pop and kiss the tip of his cock, smiling when it twitches. "I don't want you to control yourself. I want you to take what you need from me."

Not waiting for his response, I open up and suck him down as far as I can and then dig my nails into his rock-hard ass, pulling him closer to me. Jasper growls and grips my head in his hands, holding me still.

The next thing I know, Jasper is slamming his cock in and out of me, nudging the tip down my throat a little more with each thrust. I breathe through my nose and swallow around him, letting him do whatever he wants.

I find myself getting worked up with each deep stroke, my clit throbbing and aching, my nipples begging to be touched. I slip my hand between my legs and rub my dripping pussy, trembling at the sensations rushing through my body.

"Fuck. Are you touching yourself, baby? Are you wet for me? Does sucking me off make you hot?"

I moan eagerly and gasp when he pulls out of my mouth. Drawing in ragged breaths, I grip him with my free hand and jerk him off while rubbing furious circles around my clit. Once I catch my breath, I lower myself back onto his angry-looking cock with the sole mission of making him come.

Jasper's grunts turn feral as he fucks my mouth, using me for his pleasure. He thrusts into my throat once, twice, three times, then stills inside of me right before he fills me up with his cum. I swallow again and again as his dick twitches and unloads over and over.

I lick him clean and push him back slightly, guiding him to sit on the bed before climbing onto his lap and straddling him. Our lips meet in a frantic kiss, and Jasper sinks his fingers into the soft flesh of my hips, rocking me against him and making me moan.

He slides one hand from my hip to my stomach, plunging his fingers into my center. He groans when he feels how wet I am, and I bury my face into the side of his neck to muffle my cries as he thrusts two fingers into my tight channel and curls them up, stroking some magical spot that sends sparks all over my body. When Jasper grinds the heel of his palm against my clit, I come instantly.

"Fuck, yes, keep coming for me," he grunts, increasing his rhythm, making me shake and tense as wave after wave of ecstasy crashes into me and pulls me under.

I melt into his strong embrace once my orgasm finally subsides. Jasper strokes my back and murmurs sweet words in between pressing soft kisses on my forehead, temple, and the top of my head.

"Wow," I say after taking a few moments to recover.

Jasper chuckles, the warm, raspy sound wrapping around me and making me feel safe and cherished. "Agreed," he says, nuzzling into the side of my neck. "Best way to start the day. Ever."

I grin and nod, then slowly climb off of Jasper's lap. My knees shake, and Jasper grips my hips to keep me steady. "Whoa, there, I've got you."

I run my fingers through his messy hair, smoothing it off to one side so I can kiss his forehead. "Thanks," I whisper. Jasper captures my lips with his, kissing the air from my lungs. I break the kiss and take a step back, laughing when Jasper pouts. "I have a lot of studying to get done today, mister."

"Fuck studying," he grunts, reaching out for me again.

I smile but take another step back. "And you have a case to win if I remember correctly." He frowns, but I turn around and gather up some things for a shower. My room is still a complete disaster from my meltdown last night, but I'll have to clean it up later.

I'm still not sure what came over me, only that my mind was racing, my adrenaline was choking me up, and I had enough energy and anger to drop kick a mountain. And then Jasper showed up, cradling me against his chest and calming the storm until nothing but a gentle, soothing breeze remained.

"Yes, actually, you did help with that," Jasper says, pulling me back into the moment.

"Of course, I did!"

He chuckles and stands up, drawing me back in for a hug.

"Let me thank you properly," he murmurs into the shell of my ear. "Tonight. My place. Six o'clock."

I tilt my head back, peering into those green eyes full of longing. How Jasper can make me feel sexy, wanted, precious, and seen at the same time is a mystery, but I'm already addicted to it. "You better make it worthwhile. That was a really good tip," I say with a saucy smile.

"I know, baby girl. I've got a really good tip for you, too." He rubs his already hardening cock against my thigh, wagging his eyebrows.

My jaw drops open and I shove him playfully in the chest, feigning shock. "Mr. Thorn! That's very inappropriate."

"Mmhm," he growls, circling his hands around my hips and pulling my body flush with his. "Very inappropriate." His lips are on mine in the next instant, our tongues tangling together as he makes me dizzy with want. When Jasper finally pulls away, I sway toward him. He grins and kisses the tip of my nose. "Now, go wash up before I decide I need to taste you again." I'm about to tell him he can do whatever he wants, but Jasper spins me around and gives my ass a playful smack. "Go on, Faye. Wash up and get your studying done. Tonight, you're mine."

Oh, god. Yes, please.

CHAPTER NINE

JASPER

The timer for the sauce goes off, and I stir the pan before turning the heat down to a simmer. The smell of homemade alfredo sauce permeates the kitchen, and I smile to myself, knowing I've nailed this dish. Crispy, hand-breaded chicken is baking in the oven, homemade noodles are ready to be tossed into a pot of boiling water as soon as the time comes, and the garlic rosemary alfredo sauce is coming along quite nicely.

I've always enjoyed cooking. After my mom ran off, I took over a lot of the day-to-day tasks around the house while my father underwent cancer treatment. I started out with simple, staple meals, then incorporated new flavors and dishes. With my father's cancer, I also learned how to substitute certain ingredients to fit whatever diet they had him on at the time.

Over the years, I've continued to hone my cooking skills, always coming back to the kitchen when I'm stressed or overworked. It's been a while since I've made anything this involved since I just cook for one these days. I've enjoyed getting lost in the recipe and using my kitchen to its full capacity again.

A soft knock on the front door has my heart hammering in my chest. *She's here.*

I couldn't concentrate at work knowing my Faye was going to be with me tonight. I ended up leaving early, something I never do, and headed straight to the grocery store to pick up the best ingredients for dinner.

Taking a deep breath, I wipe my hands off on a kitchen towel and head to the door. I open it up at suck in a breath at the breathtaking beauty standing on my doorstep.

"Faye," I whisper, my eyes roaming up and down her body.

She's in a casual outfit, the leggings, tank top, and patterned sweater cardigan somehow making her more irresistible than any fancy dress I've seen her in. She looks soft and sweet, though the spark in her purple eyes reminds me there's so much more beneath the surface.

"What smells so good?" she asks, peeking behind my shoulder. I realize I've just been standing here, staring at her.

"Crispy chicken alfredo," I finally respond, moving to the side to invite her in. Faye only makes it a few steps inside before I close the door and pin her to it. "Missed you," I murmur before I take her lips in an all-consuming kiss.

Faye sighs when we break apart, swaying toward me with a dazed look in her eyes. I know the feeling. I lose track of time and space when we're touching.

"Wow," she breathes out, nibbling her bottom lip. "I definitely wasn't making up how good of a kisser you are." Her cheeks burn bright red at her confession, and I'm guessing she didn't mean to say that part out loud.

"Glad you approve," I chuckle, going in for another taste of her lips. Faye parts them for me, welcoming my tongue as it slides against hers. Reluctantly, I pull away from my addicting woman, grinning when she pouts. "Dinner first, playtime later," I tell her.

"Says who?" Faye asks, a playful smirk spreading across her swollen lips. "I kind of like breaking the rules. Don't you?"

I groan and roll my hips, pressing her against the wall as I rest my forehead on hers. "With you, baby girl? Fuck, yeah, I want to break all the rules." Faye nods, her nose rubbing against mine. "I don't want to rush things if you're not ready…"

"I am," she insists. "I want you, Jasper." The look in her violet eyes is full of truth and longing. It matches my own.

Faye glances down at her feet, then pulls her eyes back up to meet mine. I'm blown away by the raw need I see in them. Underneath the lust, however, is a tender vulnerability.

"I want you too, sweetheart," I reassure her. "So damn bad." I grind my aching cock against her hip, proving my point. "But not just your body. I want your heart, Faye. Are you willing to give me both?"

Faye's mouth covers mine, and she swallows down my questions in an earth-shattering kiss. She locks her ankles behind my back and wraps her arms around my shoulders, clinging to me as I lift her curvy body and carry her further into my home. I stop briefly in the kitchen, turning the oven to low and the burners to simmer. Dinner can wait. Right now, we need to feed a different kind of hunger.

Once we're in my bedroom, I untangle myself from Faye and set her on the ground, though I don't let her get very far. My hands slide up and down her curves while I kiss her soft, already swollen lips. She melts against me, her body becoming pliant as I kiss and touch and feel all of her, everything she is.

Faye runs her hands up my torso and loops her arms around my neck, pulling me back down for a punishing kiss.

I open up and take what she's offering, meeting each frantic stroke of her tongue with just as much passion and need as she's giving me.

She closes her eyes and tilts her head back, breaking our kiss so she can gulp down air. Her hands drift down to my biceps, where she grips me tightly, keeping me in place. I'm sure as fuck not going anywhere.

I can't keep my lips off of her for one goddamn second. I kiss down her neck and lick the hollow of her throat before nipping the sensitive skin there. Faye moans and digs her nails into my flesh, making me growl and grind my hard-as-fuck dick into her heat.

"Gonna lick every inch of your sexy fucking body, Faye. Then I'm gonna show you how amazing you are. How amazing I can make you feel."

Her eyes pop open, glowing with lust and hunger. Good. I plan to satisfy my woman on every level, carnal, physical, emotional, whatever the fuck she needs, she'll get it from *me* now.

She leans in at the same time I do, our lips crashing together as our need amplifies. Her desperate kiss mirrors my own, her eager hands clawing at me and begging me to give us what we both want. More.

I tear my mouth from hers just long enough to peel her shirt off. I groan at the sight of her bare breasts, and then my lips are back on her skin, trailing down her neck. "Need to be inside you, baby girl," I murmur into the shell of her ear. Faye lets out a sexy, needy little whimper as I slip my hand into her panties. My fingers part her folds and find her clit, massaging circles over the bundle of nerves. "Damn, you need it, too, don't you?"

Her cunt is fucking drenched. I don't even have to ask if she's ready, but I want to hear her say it anyway.

"God, yes, Jasper. I need you. Please, please, don't make me wait."

Hearing her beg for me is sweeter than anything I've ever experienced. A wave of pleasure rushes down my spine, drawing my balls up tight and making precum leak out of me like a damn faucet. Fuck, this woman is my undoing.

I rid her of the remaining scraps of fabric, then lift her into my arms. Tossing her onto the mattress, I strip down, adrenaline pumping in my veins and urging me to claim her right the fuck now.

Faye is spread out for me on the bed, her midnight black hair a tangled mess, her swollen lips slightly parted, her chest heaving with shallow breaths. Goddamn, she's gorgeous. And *mine.* She's all mine.

I climb on the bed and crawl up her body, kissing her thighs, torso, breasts, neck, and finally, her sweet lips. I rub my body against hers, needing that friction, needing to feel her skin against mine, needing to prove she's really here.

"I'm right here," she whispers, cupping my cheek. I stare into her otherworldly eyes, not even questioning how she read my mind. She knows me, sees me, understands me in a way no one else ever has.

I nod and take a breath, centering myself once more. Faye presses her lips to mine, her tongue seeking entrance. I give my girl everything she wants, opening my mouth to welcome her kiss.

It starts off slow, with tentative licks. I groan at her innocence but manage not to take control. Yet. Faye explores my mouth then pulls my bottom lip through her teeth, making me growl. She grins mischievously at me, and fuck, it physically pains me to hold back my orgasm. This can't be over before it even begins.

"You like knowing you have control over me?"

"Mmhm," she nods, her lips twisting into a flirty smile.

Faye gasps and then giggles as I flip our positions so she's on top. "Then take it, baby girl. Take control."

She braces herself on my chest, pushing herself up and adjusting to our new position. For a second, she looks unsure of herself, but her uncertainty vanishes when she sees my angry cock trapped between our bodies.

Faye grabs the fucker and squeezes *hard*. "Jesus Christ," I growl as I clench my fists.

She grins again, knowing exactly the kind of power she has over me. I slide my hands up her thighs and squeeze, helping her rock against me. Faye licks her damn lips as she rolls her hips, rubbing her pussy up and down my shaft. The head of my cock taps her clit and she shivers, repeating the motion.

I reach out and cup her tits, weighing them in my hands and brushing my thumbs over her nipples.

"Yes," she hisses out, her movements stuttering as she leans into my touch.

I play with her hardened peaks, twisting them and plucking them while Faye claws at my chest and rubs against me, getting herself off without me even entering her. Fuck, it's so damn hot watching her get all worked up, knowing I have so much more in store for her.

Faye's movements grow frantic as she writhes on top of me. I feel her cream dripping from her pussy, so close to coming already. A shiver runs down her spine and she holds her breath, preparing for her orgasm. I feel it pushing forward, demanding to be felt, making her whimper with each breath.

Right before it takes her under, I grip her hips and hold her still. Faye looks down at me with confusion and frustration, but then understanding dawns on her when I line myself up with her entrance. I groan when I feel her tight little channel pulse around the head of my cock.

Goddamn, her greedy little pussy is trying to suck me inside.

"Ready for me, Faye? Ready to be mine?"

She nods, her purple eyes glossed over with lust as she circles her hips, trying to get me where she wants me.

I hold her in place above me, not giving in just yet. "I need your words, baby girl. Tell me how much you want this."

"I've never wanted this with anyone else," she vows. Faye nibbles her bottom anxiously before continuing. "I've never..." She looks away from me as a pink blush creeps into her cheeks.

My heart stills in my chest. No way. I need her to tell me. I need her to say the words. "Never what, baby?"

"I've never..." She falters for a second and then gains her confidence back, looking me right in the eyes. "I'm a virgin, Jasper. But I want you, and I'm going to have you."

The determined look on her face, along with the knowledge that I'm going to be her first and last, has me growling like a fucking beast. She shocks the hell out of me by growling back and then slamming her tight as fuck pussy down on my cock.

"Jesus, fuck!" I roar, holding her still when she's fully seated. Faye whimpers, and I lean up to kiss her pain away. "You did so good, baby," I say, trying to make my voice soothing even though the most intense pressure is building up inside of me, ready to take over and fuck my woman properly. "Take it slow. We have forever."

She nods and kisses me again, her tense body relaxing as I run my hands up and down her thighs and back. I grip her ass and help her rock against me and circle her hips, finding what feels good.

"Yes!" Faye cries out, wiggling her hips and hitting her G-spot against my thick dick. She shudders and moans, rolling her sexy fucking body on top of mine, totally taking control of her pleasure.

She leans back, resting her hands on my thighs and baring her beautiful body to me while she rides my cock. I slide one hand up her torso while the other squeezes her ass and opens her up even more for me.

I cup her breast and pinch her nipple, groaning when more of her cream spills out. Jesus, I barely manage to keep it together when I look down and see where we're connected. Watching her tight, wet little cunt stretch obscenely wide to take in my many inches is something I'll remember for the rest of my life.

"That's it, Faye. That's so fucking it," I growl, moving both of my hands to her hips, jerking her up and down as I meet her thrust for thrust. Her pussy flutters around me as her muscles lock up tight.

Faye rolls forward, resting her hands on either side of my head. Her lips find mine, and we kiss and fuck like the world is burning down around us and this is our last chance to find love and passion.

She buries her face into the side of my neck and sobs as her body shakes and tightens around me. My beautiful woman bites my neck and creams all over my cock as she reaches her climax.

Something snaps inside me as I feel her orgasm devastate her.

I roll over, changing our position and fucking into that little pussy, unable to control myself. Her back bows off the bed and her legs wrap around me, holding me close. She digs her heels into my ass and claws my back, leaving her mark on me as another orgasm rattles through her.

"So good, baby," I growl before claiming her lips with my own.

I devour her, biting at her lips and spearing my tongue

inside her eager mouth, licking up every inch and then sucking on her tongue. It's a wild, messy kiss, one that matches the way I'm fucking her like a goddamn animal.

I slide one hand down her body and grip her ass cheek, changing the angle of her hips and helping her meet me thrust for thrust. My cock scrapes against her most sensitive spot with each fierce stroke.

She's breaking apart for me; I can feel it. Every time I hit the end of her, she cracks a little more, the pressure of her orgasm building and pulsing and pushing her boundaries.

My balls draw up tight as my own orgasm gathers in the base of my spine. My rhythm falters as I try to hold on, needing her to come with me. "Get there, baby, fuck, please get there. Need one more from you."

"It's too much, too much. I'm scared…"

"I've got you, Faye. Let go for me. I'm right here. Let go, love. Come for me."

She sucks in a huge breath and holds it, her whole body trembling and then freezing. Every damn muscle is pulled so tight as she clings to me with everything she has. With one last brutal thrust, we both shatter.

Faye floods my cock with her release, and I give her everything in return, my cum splashing into her throbbing pussy as she sucks down every last drop. We're both grunting, shaking, sweating as we ride that high together.

Eventually, she goes limp in my arms. I bury my face in the side of her neck and pump into her twice more before collapsing. I roll to the side and drape my freshly fucked little angel over my chest.

"Holy shit," she mumbles into my chest, her voice all scratchy as she catches her breath.

"Yeah," I agree, just as worn out and awed as she is. I mean…fuck. If I didn't know before, I definitely know now.

She's it for me. "Are you okay?" Doubt and worry rush in to take the place of euphoria. "I was so rough with--"

Faye cuts me off with a kiss. "You were perfect," she whispers against my lips before kissing me again. "Absolutely perfect. I can't wait to do it again."

I curse under my breath and tangle my fingers in her hair, angling her head to deepen our kiss. My cock is sore from how hard I fucked her, but damn if he isn't twitching to life, ready for another round.

"Gotta stop," I groan, though I can't help but kiss her again.

"I thought we liked breaking the rules," she murmurs against my lips.

I smile, giving her one last peck on the lips. "We do. But I need to make sure to feed you so I can keep your energy up. I'm not done with you yet, baby girl. Not by a long shot."

Faye blushes, and god, I love it. Love that even after all the filthy shit we just did, she's still so soft and sweet. She's perfect.

We eventually crawl out of bed, and I give Faye one of my old sweatshirts and sweatpants to wear, even though her own clothes are within reaching distance. She's drowning in them, which only makes her more adorable. The possessive beast in me wants her to wear my clothes, to get her scent all over them.

I heat dinner and serve us, chuckling when Faye's eyes go wide. "Holy crap!" she exclaims. "Wow, okay, if I knew that's what we were having for dinner, I might have changed my mind about the order of things this evening."

"Oh, yeah?" I narrow my eyes at her as I set her plate down on the table. Faye grins up at me, her brilliant eyes shining as she nods. "I don't believe you," I murmur, bending down to kiss her forehead.

Faye giggles, the sound like tinkling bells filling my soul

with pure happiness. I'll do whatever it takes to make her laugh for me every single day.

We dig into the food, and I'm pleased that it tastes just as good heated up as it did fresh. Faye moans around her first bite of food, and my dick takes notice. How is everything she does sexy and tempting?

"Jasper, this is incredible," she says in awe. "Where did you learn to cook?"

I don't want to bring the evening down by talking about my mom, so I give her a generic answer. I'll tell my girl all about the past later, but right now, I want to bask in the afterglow of what we just shared. "I taught myself. I'm glad you approve."

"Approve? Yes, most definitely. You can cook for me anytime."

"I plan on doing just that."

Faye smiles, that adorable blush tinting her cheeks. "About… us…" she starts, her features turning more serious. "Never mind. We don't have to have that conversation now." She twirls another bite of pasta on her fork and shoves it in her mouth.

"We can have whatever conversation you want," I assure her. "I know things are complicated, but we're adults. We're not doing anything wrong." Faye nods her head, but I know she doesn't totally believe me. "Look, all I know is that I crave you. Every part of you. Not just your curvy body and sparkling eyes, but your brilliant mind, your sassy little mouth, every thought in your head, every breath in your lungs… I want it as my own." Faye stares at me, her jaw dropping slightly. "Shit, I'm coming on too strong," I mutter.

"No!" Faye insists. "No, I just… you really feel that way? About me?"

Jesus, it kills me that her voice is filled with disbelief. "Yes."

Faye nods thoughtfully, then finishes off the last bite of pasta. I'm not expecting a reply. I know it was a lot to take in, but I don't regret laying my cards on the table. She needs to know I'm all in.

I stand and gather our plates, setting them in the sink to do later. Walking back over to Faye, I hold out my hand for her to take. She does, and I pull her against me, wrapping my arms around her. I kiss the top of her head before tucking it under my chin.

"Let me prove my devotion to you, Faye," I murmur. "Stay the night. I just want to hold you."

She nods against my chest, and I squeeze her tighter, wanting her to dissolve into me so I can carry her with me all the time. I step back and take her hand in mine, leading her over to the couch.

We put on some rom-com that Faye suggests and then snuggle down on the couch together. Faye curls up against my side, resting her head on my shoulder as I wrap an arm around her waist. Not even ten minutes into the movie, Faye is sound asleep. I grin to myself, satisfied that she's worn out from her orgasms and has a belly full of food.

After another ten minutes or so, I shut off the TV and scoop her up, carrying her to bed, where I strip her down and tuck her under the blankets. She barely moves, waking up only to help me get her undressed.

"Need to feel you when I hold you tonight," I whisper, kissing the tip of her nose as she nods sleepily. Curling myself around my precious Faye, I whisper how special she is to me. As sleep slowly takes over, I bury my nose in her long, black hair, breathing in her floral scent, letting it carry me off to sleep.

CHAPTER TEN

FAYE

Something brushes against my neck, then across my shoulder, causing my eyelids to flutter open. Warm sunlight streams in through a break in the curtains, and I moan as a hand slides down the side of my body, the light touch sizzling my veins.

"Morning, beautiful," Jasper whispers, his voice rough and low from sleep. I love it.

"Morning," I say softly, turning to look at him over my shoulder. Green eyes latch onto mine, darkening the longer we stare at each other.

Jasper clenches his jaw, then leans forward and kisses me with enough passion to curl my toes. He rolls over, gently guiding me to lay on my back before he kisses his way up my body. I bite my lip and spread my legs wider for him, wanting more of his skin on my skin. Wanting to be connected to him in every single way. He settles his hips in between my legs, his hot and heavy cock laying across my slit.

He begins thrusting his hips, gliding his massive dick along my folds and gathering up my honey. My nerves sizzle and pop each time the head of his cock taps my swollen clit. I swear I could come just from this, but Jasper has other ideas.

The tip of his cock nudges in my entrance, only going in a fraction of an inch. I let out a breathy moan, the slight sting only heightening my pleasure.

"Relax," Jasper whispers into my lips before kissing me slowly. He presses his forehead to mine and eases in another inch.

My tight channel pulses and sucks his huge length deeper inside me. Jasper rubs his nose against mine and then thrusts forward, swallowing my cry by kissing the air out of my lungs. He breathes life into me as he sinks his thick dick into my body.

"Ohmygod, Jasper, ohmygod..." I moan, crossing my ankles behind his back in an attempt to keep him there, so deep inside me.

"Fuck," he grits out, burying his face in my neck and biting me there as he slowly withdraws himself. Jasper slides back inside me, going even further this time, filling me up to the absolute limit and then backing out again.

He grunts and snaps his hips, slamming home in one hard thrust. I choke on the scream in my throat and bow my back off of the mattress, clawing at his skin as he hammers in and out of me. Each time he hits the end of me, my body jerks as if being electrocuted.

"Don't...stop..." I breathe out as I cling to his trembling body.

"Not a fucking chance, baby girl," he growls, bending down to suck on one of my nipples.

I gasp and whimper, but Jasper just chuckles and bites my nipple, making me buck my hips and take him impossibly deeper. We both groan, getting lost in the way our bodies fit together.

"Do you like that, Faye? Like when I bite your nipples and fuck this tight little pussy?"

"Oh, fuck…fuck, yes," I moan, barely recognizing my own voice.

"Good girl," he grunts before sucking more of my breast into his mouth.

A delicious wave of pleasure courses through me when I hear those words. *Good girl.* I want to be good for him. I want him to love me the way I already love him. I want to please him and make him happy with me. I feel my pussy tighten around his dick at the thought of him saying it again.

Jasper's thrusts become harder and faster as he licks and nips his way up to my mouth. His lips are inches from mine. All I can think about is tasting him while he fucks me. Jasper pounds into me and drags my bottom lip between his teeth, grinning when I whimper into his mouth.

"You want to be my good girl, Faye?" he whispers huskily.

I nod my head frantically, my pussy throbbing wildly as more of my cream drips out of me and soaks the sheets.

"I feel you, baby. I fucking *feel* how much you want to come. So do it, Faye, be a good girl, and come all over me."

He kisses me as he slams into me in long, rough strokes. I'm stuffed so full of his cock I can't take a full breath. I unhook my ankles from behind him and place my feet flat on the bed so I can meet him thrust for thrust.

"Christ, you feel incredible. Now let go. come for me right the fuck now, Faye."

I scream as my orgasm burns through me, all of my muscles spasming at once in the most intense moment I've ever experienced. My blood feels like sharp razor blades coursing through my veins, the pain spiking my pleasure into heights unknown.

"So goddamn beautiful, coming for me like a goddess," he

grunts, fucking me through my orgasm and then leaving me completely.

I almost cry at the loss of him, but Jasper just grabs my hips and flips me over, tugging me back so I'm on all fours. I gasp as he enters me in one hard thrust, his thighs smacking against my ass as he bottoms out, hitting me so incredibly deep.

"Jasper!" I moan, arching my back and wedging his thick dick even deeper inside me. He taps some super-sensitive spot, making my pussy convulse and my limbs shake.

"There it is," he grunts in satisfaction, gripping my hips and digging his fingers into my soft flesh.

He bounces me off his cock, hitting that spot over and over, fucking me mercilessly until I'm coming again with his name on my lips.

Jasper holds still, his cock buried inside me as my orgasm washes over me in violent waves. "Such a good girl. Give me one more, Faye. I need you to come again for me."

I whimper and squeeze my walls around his hard cock, unable to give him any words at the moment. My body is deliciously sore and used, my pussy is swollen and sensitive, and I don't think I can take anything else, but I want to give Jasper everything he wants.

One of his hands traces up my back and then tangles in my hair. He tugs my head to the side and then leans down to kiss me as he slowly begins moving in and out of my tight channel. I feel his abs tense and flex against my ass as he works his fat cock in and out of me.

I press back against him as he surges forward, earning me a sexy growl from Jasper. "That's it, baby, fuck me back, show me how much you want it."

I fist the sheets in my hands and rock back into Jasper, swallowing his hard shaft in my pussy again and again. He grabs my breasts, kneading them and holding onto me while rutting into me savagely. Jasper pinches my nipples and slams into me, each thrust pushing me closer and closer to the edge, his monster cock stretching me wider still.

"I'm…I'm…" I pant and gasp for air, barely hanging on to my sanity as he ravages my body and rips me open in powerful strokes.

"Let go, Faye. Let go for me," he rumbles. "I'm right there with you, but I need you to come first," he roars, shooting his hot cum deep inside of me.

My world erupts in pure bliss, my vision tunneling until I can't see, I can only feel. Pure light and energy are wrung from my very core as I twist in on myself and then go completely limp.

When I come to, I'm wrapped up in Jasper's arms and he's placing sweet kisses all over my face. I giggle and scrunch up my nose, trying to get away from him. He just holds me tighter and rubs his nose against mine.

"You okay, baby girl?" he whispers.

"So good," I slur, making Jasper laugh.

We lay there, a mess of tangled limbs and drying sweat, breathing the same air and snuggling in the afterglow. If I didn't know before, I definitely know now… I love Jasper. I feel safe, wanted, beautiful, and fearless.

Maybe that's why I decide to tell him about my father. I don't know if it's a good idea or not, but the words are pouring out of me almost without my permission. "My dad died when I was five."

"Faye…" Jasper murmurs, cupping the side of my face. I jerk my head away, feeling stupid for saying anything. Jasper grips my chin gently, tilting my head back so we're eye to eye. "Never hide from me, sweet girl. I want all of your secrets."

Tears sting my eyes, but I blink them away. How is this

the same person who honked at me all those weeks ago? Why is he being so good to me, and how long can it possibly last?

Shoving my doubts aside, I focus on being in the moment. Jasper and I are walking a fine line with our relationship - if it even *is* a relationship - so I want to enjoy every moment I can.

"We were out on a nature walk," I continue as Jasper rubs the back of my neck, soothing me and encouraging me to continue. "My dad loved the outdoors, and he would take me outside of the city on adventures every chance he could. That day though... we stumbled across a wounded bear cub. I didn't understand the danger, or why my father insisted I hide in an old, rotted out log."

I pause, taking a shuddering breath as I remember the horror that followed.

"I'm right here, baby," Jasper coos, his eyes full of concern.

"I curled up just in time to hear a deafening roar. The mama bear came back. I don't know what happened next. I tried covering my ears so I wouldn't hear the awful noises, but the sounds still come back to me in my dreams. My dad eventually appeared in front of my hiding spot. He said help was on the way, and he talked to me the whole time, telling me stories and singing me songs." My voice is so soft I'm not sure Jasper can even hear me, but when he nods, I know he's listening. "I had no idea... I had no idea he was bleeding out from multiple wounds." A tear slides down my cheek, and Jasper kisses it away.

"I'm so sorry, Faye," he murmurs.

"When the park rangers and police showed up, I was so scared and confused... I didn't know..." A sob gets stuck in my throat, and I squeeze my eyes shut. "By the time I was safely removed from the log with a blanket wrapped around me... he was gone. One minute he was singing the Mr.

Rogers theme song, and the next, he was just... he wasn't moving. There was so much blood..."

"I've got you," Jasper says, gathering me up in his arms and tucking me into his warm chest. "I'm so sorry, baby. So damn sorry you went through that."

I nod, taking a cleansing breath before continuing. "The doctors later explained he should have succumbed to his injuries much sooner, but the adrenaline of the situation and knowing I could have been hurt must have helped him hang on long enough to see me brought to safety." We're silent for a few moments, both of us letting the heaviness sit between us. "He sacrificed himself for me. Maybe if I insisted the paramedics treat him first or tried running for help, he would still be here..."

"Faye, sweetheart," Jasper says, cupping my face again so he can peer into my eyes. "Listen to me. Hear me when I say you are not responsible for your father's death. You were so young and in danger yourself. Your dad loved you, baby. That's what you do when you love someone; sacrifice everything to keep them safe."

I sniffle and burrow into his chest, letting the tears take over. Jasper holds me close, rocking me back and forth while I ride out the wave of emotions crashing into me.

"Your turn," I say after a few moments, my voice muffled from where I'm pressed against him. "I word vomited about the greatest tragedy in my life, so now you have to do the same."

He chuckles, combing his fingers through my hair. "Is that how it works?" I nod in confirmation, then tilt my head up to kiss his chin. "I've never had to deal with the death of a parent, though I came close once."

I rest a hand over Jasper's heart, silently letting him know I'm here and that I'll protect every piece of his heart he'll give me.

"My father was diagnosed with cancer when I was eleven."

"Really? Conner had cancer?"

Jasper nods in confirmation. "It was stage three by the time the doctors identified a spot on his left lung. The options were aggressive, but there was hope if we were willing to fight for it."

The grit and determination in his voice makes me respect him all the more. Jasper is loyal, that's for sure. I wonder what it would be like to have him by my side all the time, defending me, encouraging me, and building me up.

"And you guys did," I say in awe.

"We did. Just my father and me." I furrow my brow, not sure what he means. "My mom took off the second we got the diagnosis."

"WHAT?" I sit up so fast I nearly smash Jasper's nose with my head. "What kind of monster would *leave her husband* after he gets diagnosed with cancer? Are you kidding me?" I stare down at Jasper, stretched out on the mattress, grinning up at me. "Why are you looking at me like that? Aren't you pissed?"

"I've had years to be upset, and I still struggle to come to terms with what happened. I'm smiling because you look like you're ready to go ten rounds with my mom," he says with a chuckle.

"I definitely would. Do you have her address? We both know I have some anger I could work out on her." I ball my hands into fists and box the air, showing off my non-existent skills.

Jasper laughs and tugs me down on top of him. "I haven't bothered trying to find her, and she's never reached out. But I'm fine without her."

I nod my head, but I know his mother's betrayal hurt him

more than he's letting on. I'll just have to show him how good I can be, how I'd never abandon him.

"Good riddance," I huff out. Jasper nuzzles into the side of my neck as he curls himself around me. I love that he always wants to touch me, to hold me, to protect me from every damn thing.

"Agreed."

We lie there peacefully, feeling closer than ever. We've shared our bodies, and now, our hearts are connecting on a level I never knew possible. I want this to last forever, but I have a feeling our little bubble is going to burst soon.

So far, Jasper and I have ignored the fact that our parents will freak out if they learn about our trysts. We've ignored the age gap and the inappropriateness of being stepsiblings. The real world will come knocking soon. I just pray our bond is strong enough to survive whatever comes next.

CHAPTER ELEVEN

JASPER

I look at the clock on my desk for the tenth time in as many minutes. It's only ten forty-five, which is ridiculous. I swear it's been a year since I walked into the office this morning. I'm antsy, agitated, and aching for my Faye.

Concentrating at work has never been a problem for me. Usually, I get to the office before everyone else, have a cup of coffee in silence, then dive into work, not coming up for air until most people have gone home for the day. Lately, however, I can't wait to leave.

It's been like this for the last few weeks, ever since Faye surrendered her lucious, sweet little body to me. I no longer search for reasons to stay late, and I haven't been in the office the last three weekends, since I was busy mapping out every curvy inch of Faye with my fingers and tongue.

I was with my sweet girl last night, but I've already decided I can't make it the entire workday without seeing her again. I sent her a text this morning making plans for lunch. I have everything all planned out. My assistant arranged a picnic basket to be delivered to my office in about an hour, filled with all sorts of goodies. I told Faye to meet me in her rose garden at noon. Hopefully, I can get a little taste of my girl before heading back to the office.

God, everything about her is soft, sweet, and sassy. After feeling every inch of her, sinking inside her snug little pussy, and feeling her come all around me... Jesus, I'll never get enough. And afterwards, just holding her is satisfying and perfect in a way I can't quite understand. I need both. Crave both. Her sexy body and pure heart. Her moans of ecstasy and her whispered confessions.

And after hearing about her past a few weeks ago? The trauma and guilt she carries about her father's death? Everything in me ached to take her pain away. I hate that I wasn't there for her sooner. As irrational and crazy as it is, I'm angry at myself for not somehow finding her when she was that scared little girl trapped in that car.

She'll never know fear like that again. I'll be right here, protecting her from every bad thing. My girl will only ever know happiness and smiles from now on.

My cell phone rings, the shrill sound shattering my thoughts. I grab it off the desk, frowning when I see Monica's name flash across the screen. What the hell does she want? My father took the day off to go furniture shopping with his insufferable new wife after she begged and pleaded with him. She should be happy.

The phone rings again, and I curse under my breath before answering. "Yes?"

"Jasper! Oh, Jasper, it's awful!" Monica is hysterical, her shrill voice making it hard to understand her.

"What's going on?" I stand from my desk and pace in front of the floor-to-ceiling windows in my office.

"We were... and then... and then... he just collapsed!" She's nearly hyperventilating, her breaths short and choppy.

"Who? Who collapsed?" I'm growling at this point, but I need to get her attention so she can tell me what's happening.

"Conner!" Monica shouts miserably. She sniffles."Ambulance... took him to St. Mary's."

"I'll be right there." I hang up before she bursts into tears again. I can't handle that right now. I just need to get to my dad. What if his cancer is back? What if it's too late this time? What if he dies and the only person next to him is his awful wife?

Somewhere in the back of my head, I know these are irrational thoughts. But I'm in fight or flight mode, and nothing else matters besides getting to my dad.

Fifteen harrowing minutes later, I've fought my way through mid-day traffic and am coming to a screeching halt in the parking garage of St. Mary's. I hop out of my car, barely remembering to lock it before sprinting toward the hospital.

Once inside, I make a beeline for the information desk. The woman behind the counter looks at me with wide, concerned eyes. I'm sure I look wild and crazed. My chest is heaving with uneven breaths, and a thin sheen of sweat covers my forehead and upper lip. My hands are trembling and my jaw is clenched so tight I wouldn't be surprised if I cracked a tooth.

"Conner Thorn," I grit.

The woman furrows her brow, backing away slightly. I take a moment to compose myself, knowing I'm not going to get anywhere by grunting and acting like an asshole.

"He's my father," I say in what I hope is a calmer tone. "He was brought in via ambulance about half an hour ago."

She nods in understanding, her eyes going soft now that she knows I'm not angry. I'm panicked. "Give me a second to look him up, hon," she says soothingly. A few clicks later, and she tells me his room number. He was admitted to the ICU just a few minutes ago.

"Thanks," I tell her, dipping my head.

Making my way to the elevator bank, I press the button fifty times, even though I know it won't help it move any faster. As soon as the doors open, I step inside and sag against the wall, taking a few moments to gather my thoughts.

I can promote Danny to partner and have him take over my father's cases while he's in treatment. I'll have to hire a few more lawyers and paralegals to help out with my case-load while I watch over Dad. It'll suck spending so much time with Monica, but I don't trust her to know how to take care of a cancer patient.

The doors open with a ding, and I startle before exiting. Looking around the waiting room, I spot a frantic, sniffling Monica sitting in the corner.

"Jasper!" she calls out once she sees me. I roll my shoulders, preparing for a long, uncomfortable afternoon sitting next to Monica in these uncomfortable chairs.

"What happened?" I ask as soon as I sit down next to her. "Any updates? Has the doctor been out? Do they know if his cancer is back?"

All of Monica's hysterics stop, the concern dropping from her face, replaced with shock. "Cancer?" she whispers.

"Yes, he had lung cancer when I was a boy. He's been in remission for over twenty years now, but there's always a chance…" I trail off, not wanting to finish that thought.

"Cancer," Monica repeats. Her complexion turns ghostly white, and she dries the last of her tears.

We're both silent, the sounds of the hospital fading into the background as the gravity of the situation sinks in.

"Have the doctors been out with an update?" I ask again. Monica doesn't respond to my question. She's sitting straight up in her chair, an unreadable expression on her face. "Monica," I say more firmly. "Do you know anything about what happened?" I get that she's probably scared, but this is no time to fall apart. I need her to communicate with me, however painful that might be.

"No," she finally says, her tone a bit off. Distant. Cold.

My stomach drops, the uneasy sinking sensation prickling my nerves and stoking my anger and fear. I know what she's going to say before she even opens her mouth, but I still can't believe it.

"This changes things," Monica says slowly, her tone void of any emotion.

"Changes things?" No fucking way this is happening. Not again. And yet, I'm not surprised. Hurt, pissed, and livid on my father's behalf, but not surprised.

"Yes," Monica's answer comes, her voice even more distant, as if she's already a million miles away, free of her husband and his illness. "Yes," she says again, more firmly this time. "I didn't know… I didn't know Conner was unwell. He never disclosed that to me."

I stare at her incredulously. "What are you saying?" I know what she's saying, but I want to hear it directly from her.

"This complicates things. I'm… I'm not prepared to deal with… this," she finishes, waving her hand around.

The woman stands up, her face blank. Made of stone. She won't look me in the eye as she gathers her things.

I stare at her, my mouth hanging open. I'm having an out-of-body experience, sitting here, unable to make sense of this happening for a second time to my father.

"I need to go. I can't… I just need some space."

I can't speak, not even a single word, as I watch her walk away, heels clicking on the tile. What the actual fuck? I knew Monica was a bitch, but this…

My phone rings and I reach into my pocket, ending the call without looking. When it rings again, I silence my phone altogether. Nothing else matters right now. I won't let my dad go through this alone.

I'm not sure how much time has passed in my disbelieving, angered state, but I'm jarred out of my daze when a doctor walks into the waiting room. "Is the family of Conner Thorn here?"

I spring up out of my chair and stride toward the doctor. She's in her fifties, if I had to guess, and has a kind face.

"Yes," I say gruffly. Clearing my throat, I try again. "Yes, I'm Jasper, his son. Do you know what happened? Did he tell you about his history with cancer? Did you run labs? Elevated white blood cells can indicate infection or possibly a relapse…" I cut myself off, knowing I'm rambling. Of course, the doctor knows what elevated white blood cells are.

"Your father is going to be just fine," she says reassuringly. "He told me about his medical history, which is why we brought him up to the ICU to give him priority testing. The labs came back negative for any cancer."

Relief washes over me, the tension draining from my muscles so quickly my knees feel like they might give out. *It's not cancer. He's going to be okay.* The doctor's words repeat in my head until they finally start to sink in.

"He had some heart palpitations, which I think scared him more than anything else. His blood pressure is high, but that's also to be expected. It seems he's been under some stress lately, and had himself a good old-fashioned panic attack."

"Panic attack?"

"Has your father ever had one before?"

"Not that I know of."

The doctor nods. "They can be quite terrifying, especially if you don't know what's going on."

I grunt, taking all this information in. A panic attack. A fucking panic attack. Monica left over a panic attack.

"We've moved him out of the ICU, but I think we should keep him overnight for observation."

"Yes, good plan," I say with a nod. "Thank you, doctor." We shake hands, and then she tells me my father's new room number.

I take deep, calming breaths as I weave my way across the hospital. By the time I'm standing in front of the door to his room, the fear has mostly subsided, leaving burning rage in its place. My father doesn't deserve to be abandoned by a second wife after a health scare. What the fuck? My thoughts twist and turn ugly, the doubt in the back of my mind growing louder and louder with each passing second. At what point will Faye decide to leave? What's her limit before she walks away?

I try to convince myself she'd never leave me, but I'm not so sure. My mind races, hurt, anger, and past scars clouding my judgment. I push the door open, hoping to leave all of that behind so I can look after my father.

He's resting, his eyes closed, the steady beeping of the monitors bringing a wave of nostalgia. How many hours did I spend in hospital rooms alone with my dad? Too many to count. Sure, this time was just a scare, but what if he relapses for real? Will Faye be strong enough to stick by my side while I take care of my father? Will she understand, or will she grow irritated and resentful?

I take a few steps into the room, standing next to my dad's bed. Squeezing his hand, I plop down in the familiar, uncomfortable chair next to the bed. I'm not sure how many minutes or hours pass, but a light knock at the door has me jumping to my feet. Maybe it's the doctor with more news or possibly discharge papers.

I pull the door open, shocked to see Faye standing there. Irrational anger bubbles up from my gut, and all I can think about is Monica's betrayal. Wide, purple eyes blink up at me, but instead of making me melt like they usually do, I feel myself putting walls up to keep her penetrating gaze from affecting me.

"Jasper, oh, my god, I just talked to my mom—"

"Figures," I grunt, my stomach turning sour at the reminder of the horrible shrew. "You here just to leave, too?"

"What? No. I got here as soon as I found out what happened."

Conflicting emotions tear at my heart. Faye looks hurt, but I can't seem to process that along with all the other shit clogging up my brain.

"I just wanted to check on you both. After you didn't show up for lunch, I got worried. Is Conner okay? Can I visit him?"

"No." My response is automatic, my voice harsh. "Family only. Since your mother is probably already looking up divorce lawyers, you don't qualify anymore."

"Jasper, you don't mean that," she whispers, her shoulders dropping.

"I do. You need to leave." The words taste bitter on my tongue, but I'm no longer in control of what I'm saying. I need to protect myself and my father from any more damage.

She stares at me for a long moment, then tears fill her eyes. I hate myself, but I can't seem to move or even speak. I'm frozen, stuck between wanting to comfort her and needing to push her away.

"Okay," she finally whispers.

Faye gives me one last, lingering look, hurt etched in her

features. My heart feels like it's being stabbed with a thousand tiny needles, but still, I stand my ground. She backs away, then turns on her heel and power walks toward the exit. I see her shoulders shaking, and I know I made her cry. Guilt, fear, and stubborn anger choke me up, and I close the door, resting my forehead against the cool wood.

"Idiot."

I turn around at the sound of my father's voice, rushing over to his side.

"Dad. How are you feeling? Do you know what happened?"

He nods his head and motions for me to sit down. "Well, at first, I thought I was having a heart attack," he says with a chuckle. "Should have known it was my body telling me enough is enough. Panic attack, the doc said."

"Yeah. I had no idea you were under such stress. I can help with clients, you know that. Whatever you need."

He smiles at me and nods. "I know, Son. It has nothing to do with work." He sighs heavily, leaning his head back against the pillow. "Monica... she's not who I thought she was."

"No shit," I grunt.

Dad chuckles again. "Can't blame an old man for wanting to find love and being blind to the flaws," he says ruefully.

I grunt, thinking of Faye. I know if she stuck around for long enough, I'd find flaws. At least, that's what I'm telling myself to justify the way I just treated her. "Well, in that case, maybe you won't be too heartbroken to hear Monica left." There's no good way to break the news to him, so I decide just to lay it all out there.

Dad grunts. "I'm not surprised, though I'd be lying if I said it didn't sting a bit." I squeeze his hand, and he squeezes mine back. "But enough about me. You're being a goddamn fool."

I jerk my head back, shocked at the force behind his words. "What are you talking about? Are you sure you're feeling alright?" Maybe they put him on some meds that made him loopy or something.

"I'm fine. You, on the other hand, I'm worried about. Why did you kick Faye out?"

I stare at him, slack-jawed, before sputtering out an answer. "She's not family. Not anymore."

"Bullshit."

"Excuse me?"

"Boy, I raised you. I know you. And I'm no fool. Your legal library is twice the size of mine. No way you needed to borrow a single book, let alone multiple," he says with a wink.

"What are you saying?"

"That you're head over heels for that girl, and you're screwing it all up by letting the past get in the way."

"I'm not… look, it's… complicated."

"It doesn't have to be. Tell me you don't love her."

"It's too soon to say that."

"Boo, next excuse."

I grunt at him and wipe a hand down my face. "I can't love her. What if she leaves? What if I get too attached and she walks out, leaving me devastated?"

"That's still not a no, Jasper. Why are you fighting this so hard?"

"Why are you?"

"Because I've seen the way you look at her, like she's your reason for breathing. And that girl is crazy about you, too. She looks at you like you hung the moon and lit the stars just for her. I've never experienced that, but I want you to have it."

"Dad…"

"Tell me you don't love her. Tell me you're not hurting right now just thinking about the harsh words you said."

"That's not fair."

He doesn't say anything. He just stares at me expectantly.

"I do feel like shit, but about love…" I think back on our first meeting, how she aggravated me and turned me on at the same time. Her sassy little mouth and sweet blush. Her purple eyes, kind heart, and love of flowers. Her wit, charm, and vulnerability. "Fuck," I mutter. "I love her. I love her so damn much."

My dad nods, a big grin plastered on his face. "I know," he says smugly. "Now, what are you going to do about it?"

"Fuck," I curse again, realizing what an ass I've been. "I need to get her back."

CHAPTER TWELVE

FAYE

"Can I get you some more tea?" Sarah asks, getting up to refill her mug.

"I'm okay, thanks," I tell her with a weak smile.

Sarah frowns at me, concern mounting in her eyes. I turn my gaze back to my half-empty mug of tea, avoiding eye contact.

We're silent for a few moments while Sarah fixes her drink. When she sits down at the kitchen table right next to me, I know we're going to have a talk. *The* talk. The one I've been avoiding for the past week since moving in with Sarah and Dylan.

"It might help just to get it all out there," she says softly. "A good old-fashioned purge of emotions. You know I'd never judge you, and once all the ugly little pieces are out of your mind and heart, we can start to put your life back together."

I continue to stare into my mug of tea, nodding my head a few times. I know she's right. I've been crashing with my bestie and her man ever since my mom kicked me out, and I owe her an explanation.

Sighing, I gulp down my cold tea and turn to Sarah, who gives me an encouraging smile. "So, I'm guessing you already figured out Jasper and I are together."

Sarah nods her head, a spark of hope in her eyes.

"Well, we *were* together. Until…" I suck in a breath, pushing my tears back. I've already cried an ocean's worth these last seven days.

"It's okay. You can tell me," Sarah says, her hand covering mine.

"I'm not even sure myself what changed," I whimper pathetically, thinking about that day. "We were going to have a picnic for lunch, but he never showed up. I called and called, but he never answered. Then my mom came home hours early from her shopping excursion, alone. She told me Conner collapsed and was at the hospital."

Sarah nods and hands me a few tissues. God, I'm such a mess.

"Is he okay?"

"I don't even know!" I cry. "I panicked when she said he was in the hospital. He had cancer years ago, and I was worried he'd had a relapse. I begged my mom to tell me which hospital he was at. I think that's what tipped her off," I say with a sigh.

"About Jasper?" Sarah asks.

I nod in confirmation. "Yeah. She gave me this disapproving look, which I thought I was immune to. This was something else. Something final. Then she called me a perverted slut and told me to get the hell out of her house."

"That bitch!" Sarah says forcefully, banging her fist on the table. "I knew things were bad with your mother, but I had no idea you were living like that."

"It hasn't been too bad," I hedge.

Sarah narrows her eyes at me, and I roll mine at her.

"Fine, we had a pretty big fight over an old sleazeball date she arranged."

"And that's when Jasper held you, right? He can't be so bad if he was there for you during everything."

"That's just it! He was perfect. Sexy, sweet, and just arrogant enough to be charming." I try pulling my mind back, but I can't seem to help picturing Jasper's messy hair, his piercing green eyes that crinkle slightly at the corners, and his smile. It took me a long damn time to finally see it, and I feel hollow inside knowing I'll never experience his smile again.

"And then...?" Sarah prompts.

"I figured out where Conner was and headed that direction. When I got to his room, Jasper came to the door and kicked me out. Said we weren't family anymore. He was so... angry. Betrayed." Remembering Jasper's harsh words, I grit my teeth, agony giving way to anger. "But I didn't do anything!" I seethe. I've been oscillating from heartbroken to bitter. It's exhausting. "How could he toss me out like that? What did I do wrong?"

"Nothing," Sarah says fiercely. "You didn't do anything wrong."

We're quiet once more, letting the words sit between us while we figure out what happens next.

"You said Conner had cancer before," Sarah starts, her voice hushed like she's respecting the silence. "I'm sure that was terrifying for Jasper. Not that there's any excuse for the way he treated you, but maybe he was lashing out?"

I shrug my shoulders. "I guess. But he hasn't apologized. He hasn't reached out. If it was all just an emotional reaction, wouldn't he have calmed down by now?"

Sarah considers my words, her eyes assessing as she looks at me. "Neither one of us had a great example of how to love," she says, seemingly out of the blue.

I snort out a sarcastic laugh. "Yeah, no kidding."

"When we don't know how to love, we do the best we can, even if it comes from a broken, distorted place." She pauses, gathering her thoughts before continuing. "Look, all I know is that I loved Dylan, but my love was coming from a place of fear that he would leave. I didn't trust that he'd choose me, so I made it easy for him and left."

"But I thought Jasper would choose me," I say through sniffles.

"Did he think *you* would choose *him?*" Sarah asks.

"What do you mean? Of course, I would choose him. I did. I showed up at the hospital, didn't I?"

"I know, I know," Sarah concedes. "I guess all I'm saying is maybe Jasper is trying to love from a broken place. Maybe he's a little like me, and he wanted to cut ties before his worst fear came true - you leaving."

I rest my head in my hands, trying to keep all the jumbled thoughts inside. There's no doubt Jasper has been hurt before. His mother abandoned him and his father at a time they needed more support than ever. But I'm not like that. I thought he knew me. It still hurts like hell that he didn't trust me, that he wouldn't even give me a chance to talk it out.

"That doesn't change the fact that he hasn't contacted me all week," I grumble, my voice muffled by my hands.

Sarah pats my shoulder soothingly, letting me know she's here for me. "Don't give up on him yet, okay?"

I'm about to tell her I don't have much of a choice, but Dylan walks into the kitchen. His whole face lights up when he sees Sarah, and she beams right back at him. God, these two are adorably, nauseatingly in love.

"Hey," Sarah sings, standing to give him a hug.

"Hi, baby," Dylan says, kissing the top of her head. "Faye," he says in greeting, nodding in my direction.

"How's Reed doing?" Sarah asks.

I've been privy to the latest drama between Reed Landis,

the dean of our college and Dylan's best friend. He got custody of his six-year-old niece a few months ago and has struggled to find and keep a nanny. From what I've gathered, this latest one has been around for longer than the others, but she also seems to be the most headache-inducing.

Dylan chuckles and shakes his head. "He's at his wit's end, though he's completely wrong about the reason why the nanny is so upsetting." Dylan presses a kiss to Sarah's forehead, then they break apart and join me at the table.

"Is she giving him trouble?" Sarah asks.

"Not exactly. I know she's a bit more... creative and care-free than Reed is, which is bound to cause some friction, but truthfully, I think the man is in love with her," Dylan says with a smirk.

"Aw!" Sarah exclaims. "He deserves a good woman. I'm happy for them."

"Yeah, if they don't kill each other first," Dylan adds. "Seems the two are playing a game of chicken over who's more stubborn."

"Oh, man, it's going to be so good when they finally get together," Sarah says with a giggle. Dylan grins at her, the love in his eyes too much for me to take.

Sarah wants to see a happily ever after for everyone now that she's found hers. Me? I'm starting to be more realistic about such things. Not everyone gets a lifetime with their true love. Some of us only get a few weeks.

My stomach churns violently, and I clamp my mouth shut, dashing to the bathroom just in time to empty what little contents I had in my stomach. I kneel in front of the toilet, tears and snot streaming down my face. I don't want to think about what this means. I try to ignore the fact that this is the fourth morning in a row I've gotten sick. It usually passes after an hour or so, which only confirms my suspicions.

A knock on the door filters through my thoughts, scattering them to the corners of my mind. "Faye? Are you alright? Can I get you a glass of water or anything?"

Dammit. So far, I've been able to avoid Sarah and Dylan in the mornings, so they don't know about my morning sickness. They also don't know I bought a pregnancy test yesterday and have been too scared to take it.

"I'm good," I tell my friend, though my voice is scratchy from being sick. "Sorry to interrupt breakfast."

"Psh, that doesn't matter. I'm worried about you."

I stand and clean myself up, washing my face and brushing my teeth. Opening the door, I see Sarah leaning against the wall across from the bathroom. "I think I'm just going to lay down for a bit," I say, hoping she doesn't press the issue.

Sarah frowns but nods, her eyebrows furrowed in concern.

I drag myself to the guest bedroom I've been staying in and head straight for the ensuite bathroom. Pulling out the pregnancy test from the bottom of my makeup bag where I hid it, I tear the damn thing open and read the instructions.

Three anxiety-inducing minutes later, I check the test. And then recheck. Yup, two lines are still staring back at me, loud and clear.

My legs give out and I sink to the floor, curling my knees up and wrapping my arms around them. I'm about to be a homeless single mom at age twenty-one. How the hell did this happen?

I allow myself ten minutes of freaking the fuck out, questioning my life choices, and worrying about the future. And then, I pick myself up, dust myself off, and do what I need to do. Go to class. My education is more important than ever if I plan on supporting myself and my baby.

I'm having a baby.

It doesn't feel real. It's not at all how I thought my life would go, and while a part of me is overwhelmed that I'm all alone in this, another part of me feels like it's sparking to life. My need to love and protect my child is already surging through my veins.

Three excruciating hours later, I'm finally done with my last lecture of the day. I slip out of the classroom and throw my backpack over one shoulder, shielding my eyes from the sun as I step outside.

"Faye."

I whip my head around, my pulse racing at the sound of that familiar voice. It's so damn bright out it takes a few seconds of me blinking to finally focus.

"Jasper?" I murmur as his large frame steps closer, blocking out the sun.

He's all I see. Intense green eyes, smooth lips, a sharp jawline covered in stubble. The longer I look at him, the more details I pick up. There are dark circles under his eyes like he's been sleeping about as much as I have this last week. Jasper has traded his normally crisp and clean suit for jeans and a white t-shirt. I've never seen him this casual, and I hate to admit he looks just as hot as he does in his expensive suits.

"Faye," he says again, his right hand twitching at his side. He balls it up into a fist, then shoves it into his pocket as if he doesn't trust himself not to touch me.

"Um... hi?" I say awkwardly, tucking some hair behind my ear. What do you say to your ex-stepbrother/lover? Especially when you just found out you're pregnant with their kid?

My stomach sinks, and tears cloud my vision, but I swallow thickly and adjust my backpack, fiddling with the strap so I don't have to look at him.

Jasper's large, warm hand gently covers mine where I'm

tugging at my backpack. "Don't be nervous around me, sweetheart," he whispers.

His endearment for me is almost my breaking point. I sniffle, cursing myself for being weak.

"Baby, please don't cry."

"I'm not," I tell him with more strength than I thought I had. I jerk my hand away from his, wrapping my arms around my torso.

Jasper sighs and runs a hand through his hair. "I deserve that," he mutters. "Can I show you something? Then if you want to go home, I'll take you."

Home.

I squeeze myself tighter, trying to hold everything in until I can fall apart in private. "That won't be necessary," I tell him, straightening my back. "Will you just tell me if Conner is okay? Then you never have to speak to me again." I tip my chin up, finally looking him dead in the eye. He looks pained by the thought of never seeing me again, but that doesn't make sense.

"Never speak to you..." he repeats softly, shaking his head. "That would fucking kill me, Faye. Conner is much better. He had a panic attack."

I nod, relieved he's okay.

"Come with me. Let me show you something."

"I don't understand you!" I finally blurt, confused, hurt, and angry. I refuse to be yanked around by the man who broke my heart.

"I know, sweetheart. I know. I messed up. I'm so damn sorry. Give me one hour. Let me apologize correctly. Let me show you how our life could be together."

Maybe it's the pregnancy hormones or my exhaustion, but I don't want to fight him anymore. Jasper holds out his hand, and I hesitate for a moment before placing my trembling hand in his.

"Thank you," he murmurs, squeezing my fingers. "Thank you for giving me a shot, baby."

"You better make it good," I huff as he leads me to his car.

Jasper smirks, and yup, it's just as potent as it's always been. "Only the best for you from now on, Faye. I promise."

CHAPTER THIRTEEN

JASPER

I try taking deep breaths as I pull into my driveway. Hyperventilating right now would ruin all the planning and work that went into this last week. It killed me being away from my beautiful girl, but everything had to be perfect. How could I ask for her back when I have nothing to offer?

Faye looks at me across the console, her brows furrowed.

"Do you trust me?" As soon as the words are out of my mouth, I want to snatch them back. Of course, she doesn't trust me.

My girl shocks the hell out of me by responding, though her voice is so soft I almost don't hear it. "I want to."

God, those words break my heart and give me hope at the same time. It's a starting point, and that's more than I deserve.

I smile at Faye before jumping out of the car and rushing to her side. I help her out, not letting go of her hand even after she's done. Guiding us around to the back of my property, my heart thrashes in my chest, anxiety tightening my lungs and making it hard to breathe. What if this is a mistake? What if she thinks it's stupid or that I'm trying to buy her love? What if–

"Oh, my god," Faye breathes out. "Oh, my god, Jasper… is that a greenhouse?"

"It's for you. I researched the proper glass, frames, and temperature regulators. It's not completely done. I had some help for the first two days, but then my buddies had to continue their actual construction jobs. I wanted you to pick out the plants, which means I couldn't buy the soil yet. I had no idea there were so many different kinds, and I didn't know what you wanted." I finish my word vomit, my stomach in knots.

Looking over at Faye, she has her hand clamped over her mouth, tears glistening in her violet eyes. Fuck, is she going to run away from me? Throw a stone through every window in the greenhouse? I deserve it.

Instead, Faye turns to me, dropping her hand to take mine. I feel like I can breathe for the first time since I kicked her out of the hospital.

"You built me a greenhouse?"

"I had help. And we can change anything you want. I was thinking about adding a separate room that's airtight. The articles I read talked about doing cross-pollination in a confined space. It sounded creative and like something you'd want to experiment with. But we don't have to if you hate that idea." God, I can't stop rambling.

"You built me a greenhouse," she says again.

"It's too much, isn't it?" I mutter, feeling like an idiot.

Rubbing the back of my neck, I try to come up with a new plan to woo Faye. The greenhouse was too much, but maybe a fancy date would be better. Start out slow. Then, after a few months–

I'm jarred out of my spiral by Faye throwing her arms around my waist. I'm too shocked to respond for a second, but then I wrap her up in my embrace, holding her as close to me as possible. This has to be a good sign, right?

"Say something," I murmur into the top of her head. "What are you thinking? Do I have a shot with you, baby girl?"

Faye untangles herself from me, but I keep a hold on her hips, planting her solidly in front of me. I never want to let her go.

"I can't believe you did all this. Why? I thought you didn't want me anymore."

"Jesus," I grunt, pulling her back into my arms. "I'm so sorry, Faye. I was an idiot, a fact my father pointed out as soon as you left."

"What?" Her head pops up, those purple eyes full of shock.

"Yeah, apparently, I didn't give my old man enough credit. He knew I was in love with you from day one. I just needed to get over myself and stop being a fool."

"You love me?" Faye gasps.

I nod, cupping her cheeks in my hands. "So damn much."

"B-but… you never reached out. You didn't call or text. I had no idea if Conner was okay or what happened to you. I hated that, Jasper."

"I know, and I can't apologize enough. I know I did wrong, baby girl. I realize now I should have gone to you right away, but I…" I let out a breath and look up to the sky, gathering my thoughts. "I don't have anything else to offer you," I admit. "But I thought if maybe I had a greenhouse, you could picture yourself here, with me."

"Jasper," she says softly. "I love the greenhouse, and it's the most thoughtful thing anyone has ever done for me. But what I really want is you. Your heart. Your trust. Your… loyalty." She whispers the last part, and it fucking guts me.

"You have it all. Everything. Fuck, I'm so sorry for the

way I treated you. I don't have an excuse for my behavior, only the promise that I'll never do it again."

"You were loving from a broken place," Faye murmurs.

"What?"

"Something my friend Sarah said. We both have wounds, and we were trying to love each other from a broken place." I nod my head, encouraging her to continue. Did she just say she loves me? "But I'm ready for the real thing if you are. I'm ready to trust you if you can trust me, too."

"Yes," I say, nearly cutting her off. "Always. Forever." Faye gives me a tentative smile, but then doubt clouds her eyes. "What is it?" I ask.

"I, um… I need to tell you something first. It might change things."

"Not possible."

"Will you just listen?" She rests her balled up fists on her hips. So damn adorable when she's giving me shit. I grin and nod my head. I love seeing her sassy side come out. "So, I just found out this morning," she starts. "Jasper, I'm pregnant."

The world stops spinning. My breath leaves my lungs all at once, and I struggle to remain upright under the weight of this amazing news.

"Pregnant," I whisper.

Faye sniffles and I realize I haven't said anything reassuring. I'm still struggling to wrap my head around everything that's happened. Am I really getting everything I've ever wanted?

I drop to my knees, hitting the dirt as I look up at my precious girl. "That's incredible news, baby girl. I'm so happy," I tell her with all the love and joy I feel in my soul.

"Yeah?" she asks tentatively.

"Hell, yes. Oh! Let me prove it to you." I can't believe I almost forgot the most important part. Sealing the deal. I dig into my pocket, pulling out the little blue velvet box containing the ring I bought a few days ago.

"Jasper..."

I take the rose gold diamond ring out of the box and slip it on Faye's ring finger before she has a chance to respond. "Marry me," I command.

Her lips quirk up on one side, sending sparks up and down my spine. "Want to try that again?"

I chuckle, most of the tension leaving my muscles. "Faye, my sweet girl, will you please forgive me for being a selfish ass and let me spend the rest of our lives making it up to you?"

Faye nibbles on her bottom lip then nods her head, the first tears rolling down her flushed cheeks. "Yes."

I shoot up off the ground and scoop my woman up off her feet, carrying her inside our home. She kicks her feet out then snuggles against my chest, making me feel invincible. I sit down on the couch, tucking Faye into my side.

"Need to hear you say it again," I whisper, weaving a hand through her hair and cupping the back of her neck. "Tell me you love me. Tell me you'll never leave."

"I love you, Jasper."

I groan and tip my head back, letting her words soothe and heal me.

"I love you forever and always. Me and our baby."

I snap my head back down, grinning at my girl. "Our baby," I whisper, loving the way she blushes. I lean down and kiss her cheeks because how can I not?

I kiss her again before trailing my lips down her jaw, her neck, her collarbone. I gently push her back so she's lying down on the couch and continue my trail of kisses down between her perfect tits. I can't wait to see them swell up. Fuck, now that I'm thinking about it, I can't wait to see her pregnant.

My lips trail down her ribcage and I lift her shirt and kiss her belly. Resting my forehead there, it finally clicks into place. This is everything. We're starting a family together. She's fucking mine, all mine, and now she's tied to me in every way.

I close my eyes when I feel Faye's fingers weave into my hair and massage my scalp. "You're growing my baby in there," I whisper against the soft skin of her belly before kissing it again.

"Yeah," she giggles.

I look up, hoping to see that sparkle in her eyes again. I hate that I ever made her think I would ditch her for any reason, let alone something as life-changing as this. To my delight, she's smiling down at me, a real, genuine smile that warms me up.

"That's so fucking sexy," I growl. And it is. Jesus, I want nothing more than to be inside her right this fucking second.

"It is?"

Instead of answering her, I hook my thumbs into the waistband of her shorts and panties, peeling both of them down her legs to reveal her perfect, pink little pussy. Without any warning, I dive into her sweet perfection, licking up her slit and circling her clit.

Faye cries out in surprise at the unexpected invasion, but soon I taste her arousal. I suck and lick and nip at her folds, her thighs, her hard little clit. She's soaking me, my face sloppy with her juices. I fucking love it. She comes hard and fast, her pussy pulsing around my tongue as I lap up her release.

"Again," I growl into her tight, hot cunt.

Faye moans as her hips buck, grinding herself against my mouth. I grab her hips and pull her even closer until I'm suffocating inside her sweet heat. I lick her clit again and again until my tongue is numb. She sucks in a huge breath and then cries out her climax. I crawl up her body and kiss her, hard and deep. She takes everything I give her, moaning at her taste in my mouth.

Not wasting any more time, I rip her flimsy t-shirt down the middle, loving the fact that she's not wearing a bra. Faye giggles at first but then moans as I suck one tit into my mouth. She bows her back off of the couch, thrusting her chest further into me. I kiss and lick my way to her other breast and give it the same attention.

I leave her briefly, only to unbuckle my belt and pull off my jeans and underwear. I grab one of her ankles and place it over the back of the couch while the other one rests on my shoulder, spreading her wide open for me. Looking down at this stunning woman, chest heaving, pussy dripping, eyes fogged over with lust, I can't help but groan.

"So fucking beautiful. God, you're perfect, Faye."

I line myself up and enter her tight little channel in one long thrust. I growl at the sensation of her silky heat wrapped around my aching cock. Faye throws her head back and claws at the couch cushions. She gushes for me, making it easy to slide in and out of her. I pick up my pace, needing her to come again, needing to show her how much I love her, how I'm never leaving her.

"Mine," I grunt as I piston in and out of her.

"Y-yours, oh, fuck, fuck, Jasper, I can't hold on…"

"Let go, Faye. I love watching you fall apart." Her orgasm slams into her, causing her body to shake and convulse beneath me. "Jesus Christ, that's it."

I fuck her through her orgasm as she whimpers and writhes. I can't hold off much longer, but I don't want this to end. I want to be inside her forever.

I pull out of her as she moans, snapping her eyes open and searing me with her lustful gaze. Standing up, I pull her into me and spin her around, guiding her to lean over the arm of the couch. I grab her hair and push her forward onto her elbows. I press my cock against her soaking wet pussy, her previous releases dripping down her thighs. I tease her as I wait for exactly the right moment.

My cock spurts cum at the sight of Faye bent over the couch for me. I grit my teeth and take a calming breath, trying to keep my shit together. I need her to surrender to her pleasure one more time. Ten more times. A thousand more times. But for now, I'll settle for her fourth orgasm of the day.

"Jasper, please, please get inside of me."

"Fuck, baby, you know I'll always give you what you need."

I tease her a little longer, rubbing my cock up and down her slit. When she starts shaking and whimpering, I slam my thick dick deep inside her, triggering another orgasm. I roar with pride over how much pleasure I can give my woman and how well she takes all of my many inches.

My hips snap as I buck and thrust, my heavy balls slapping her pussy. Every time we join together, we make the most obscene and glorious wet smacking sounds. It makes me impossibly harder.

I can't tell if she's having one long orgasm or if she's had five more, but her pussy has been squeezing and snapping around me the entire time. I loop my arm around her waist, holding her up just as she starts to collapse. I give one more hard thrust before fucking exploding inside of her.

It's so intense, so fucking everything. I keep emptying into her, coming harder than I ever have. Each rope of cum feels like it's taking a part of my very soul, draining me and pouring more of me into her. I'll give her everything. There is no me without her.

Finally, fucking *finally*, I'm completely spent. I curl my

body over hers, covering her back with my front as I kiss the nape of her neck, loving the salty taste of her sweat.

Faye is shaking in my arms, panting and sweating and well-fucked.

"You doing okay, baby?" I whisper into her ear.

"I...fuck," she breathes out. "S-so good. Can't feel my legs."

I chuckle and then stand up, pulling out of her swollen, soaked pussy. Spinning her around again, I scoop Faye up into my arms. She's a fucking rag doll, and I chuckle again, kissing her forehead before collapsing on the couch with her in my lap.

She curls up into my chest and rests her head in the crook of my neck.

"I fucking love you, baby girl. Nothing will ever change that. You are my family, my home, my whole damn world. I'll do whatever I can to prove that to you."

She nods and kisses my neck. "I know," she whispers into my skin. "I know that. You're my...you're my family." Her voice cracks on that last word, making me hold her even tighter. "I was just scared. But I want this more than anything. And I want it with you."

We sit like that for god knows how long, the air thick with sex and promises of forever. It's the most perfect moment.

"So, when are you moving in?" I ask, breaking the silence. Faye giggles, and I smile, loving the sound of it echoing around our home.

"You sure you won't get tired of me hanging around all the time?"

She's half teasing, but I hear the thread of vulnerability in her voice. "Never," I vow. "Let's get your stuff right now."

The playful smile drops from her face. "About that..." Faye takes a deep breath and curls into my chest. "My mom sort of kicked me out after… well, after she figured out we'd been together. I've been staying with a friend, trying to figure out my next steps."

"Faye, oh, sweetheart… I had no idea. Fuck. I'm so sorry. I would have come for you sooner."

"I'm okay," she assures me, but my heart is still raw and aching. I can't believe she forgave me after everything.

"From now on, you'll be more than okay. You'll always know how loved you are, how precious you are to me. I had no idea how much I was missing out on until you crashed into my life."

"Hey, now, I never crashed into you!"

"Right, just cut me off, then," I say as I tickle her sides. Fay erupts into laughter, grabbing my shoulders to steady herself. "I love you with my whole damn heart, Faye."

"Good. You better. 'Cause mine already belongs to you."

I rest my forehead on hers, then cover her heart with my hand. I'm thankful for each beat I feel, knowing how close I was to losing her. "I'll protect it, love. I'll protect all of you. Forever."

"I like the sound of that," she sighs.

I nod, then close my eyes, picturing the rest of our lives together. I can't fucking wait to get started on our happy ending.

EPILOGUE

Faye

"Katie, look at your sunflower! It's almost as tall as you now!" I tell my six-year-old daughter.

She grins, her toothy smile and green eyes shining up at me. "And soon it will reach the sky!" she exclaims, lifting her arms and waving them around. "And then I can climb it and reach the giant in the clouds and steal his gold!"

I laugh, pruning back some of the dried leaves from the sunflower. "I think you've got your fairy tales mixed up, honey. Only magic beanstalks reach the sky," I tell her matter-of-factly.

Her eyes go round, and I can see the little wheels turning in her head. "Mommy, can we get a bean sock?"

"A beanstalk?" I correct. She nods enthusiastically. "Maybe when you're a little older."

Katie rolls her eyes and huffs out a breath. She's so dramatic. I wonder where she gets it from.

"Go check on your little brother," I tell her, tugging lightly on one of her adorable pigtails. "He's over by the strawberries."

She smiles once again, the disappointment of the beanstalk a distant memory. I watch her chubby little legs carry her to Gray, our four-year-old. He's my quiet kid, always so serious. Much like his father used to be. Katie is absolutely in love with her little brother and does whatever she can to get him to smile.

I hear footsteps behind me, the familiar, comforting scent of pine needles wrapping around me seconds before Jasper's arms circle my waist.

"Morning, beautiful," he whispers into the shell of my ear before kissing the side of my neck.

"Morning, sleepyhead," I tease, settling back against my husband.

"Who's fault is that? I seem to remember someone keeping up half the night, wiggling your curvy little body against mine and driving me crazy."

I shrug, a grin pulling at my lips at the memory of the intense way we made love last night. "Sorry, not sorry."

Jasper chuckles, and we both watch our children from one side of the greenhouse, smiling as they dig around in the dirt and pick fresh strawberries.

We've expanded the greenhouse over the years, adding some fruits and veggies to the array of roses and other flowering plants. We went to my favorite gardening shop at the beginning of the summer, and I had the kids pick out their favorite flowers to grow in the greenhouse. Katie wanted sunflowers, and Gray was dead set on strawberries. They've loved being more involved in gardening, and I've loved having them with me all the time.

I mostly work from home these days since I have my own lab set up in the greenhouse. Right now, I'm working on developing and breeding a kind of rose that doesn't have thorns. The trick is to get the flowering part to be a pleasing color. Right now, it's just a tiny, greenish-brown bud. But I'll keep working on it. I love what I do, and I love how supportive Jasper has been.

We got married a week after he proposed. Jasper said we could wait and have a huge wedding, but I didn't care about all of that. I just wanted him. We had a small, intimate ceremony with just the officiant, Conner, and Sarah as our witnesses. It was simple, pure, and perfect, just like I wanted our love to be. So far, it has been. That's not to say we haven't had our share of ups and downs, but through it all, we chose each other.

"What are you thinking about, sweetheart?" Jasper asks as he nuzzles into my neck.

"You," I sigh, leaning against his shoulder. "I love my life with you."

Jasper presses another kiss to my neck, then one on my temple. "I love hearing you say that, Faye. I want you to have everything you've ever dreamed of."

"You're all I want. You make me so happy."

Jasper hums in approval, and I turn my head just in time to receive the kiss I knew he had waiting for me. His lips meet mine, and I get swept away by his tongue, his teeth, every part of him. He's consuming me, claiming me, and loving me, just like he promised he always would.

"Eww!" Katie whines.

Gray follows suit, blowing a raspberry in our direction. Jasper laughs, and I giggle at our kids.

"Show me what you two have been working on," Jasper says, giving me one last squeeze before kneeling to get on the same level as Katie and Gray.

Katie chatters away, while Gray nods, always so stoic. Jasper listens to every word as our kids explain gardening to him. He looks over his shoulder, his green eyes catching mine. I smile at my husband and he winks back at me.

Yeah, I'd say I got my happily ever after.

* * *

THE END

Find out if Reed and his nanny end up together in Secret Desire!
Curious about Dylan and Sarah? Get their story in Secret Obsession!

ALSO BY CAMERON HART

Check out my other popular series and books!

Mountain Men Romance:

Men of Blackthorne Mountain Series

Bear's Tooth Mountain Men Series

Mafia, MC, & Bodyguard Romance:

Moscatelli Crime Family Series

Chaos MC series

Savage Ride

Watchdog Protection, Inc.

Curvy Girl Romance:

Curvy Temptations Boxset

Secret Temptations Series

Infinity

Claiming His Babygirl

At First Sight

Designed by Fate

My Heart & Soul

Finding Her Strength

1012 Curvy Way

Cowboy & Small Town Romance:

Roped in by Love Series

Small Town Love Boxset

Where I Belong

ABOUT THE AUTHOR

Cameron Hart is a USA Today bestselling author of contemporary romance. She writes books with lots of heat, plenty of sweet, and just enough drama to keep things interesting.

Sign up for Cameron Hart's newsletter to get a free novella!

Join Cameron Hart's street team to receive ARCs & help spread the word about new releases.

instagram.com/cameron.hart.author

amazon.com/Cameron-Hart/e/B07Q62HF6L

bookbub.com/authors/cameron-hart

tiktok.com/@cameron.hart.author